DEXTER

A CROSS TO BEAR BOOK 2

KATHI S. BARTON

World Castle Publishing, LLC
Pensacola, Florida
Copyright © Kathi S. Barton 2022
Hardback ISBN: 9798849742465
Paperback ISBN: 9781958336663
eBook ISBN: 9781958336670
First Edition World Castle Publishing, LLC, September 5, 2022
http://www.worldcastlepublishing.com
Licensing Notes
Cover: Karen Fuller
Editor: Karen Fuller

Prologue

Sunny didn't mind people—just not in clumps. She supposed that calling them clumps was better than calling them herds. But they sort of did remind her of cattle the way they mooed when they were upset—well, whined. And they complained all the time. She'd not met a single person on this trip who hadn't complained about something, even the weather being too hot. Damn it all to hell, people. It's summer! It's supposed to be hot. She'd bet those same people were surprised when it turned cold during the winter months.

A clump of people was just ahead of her, and she had to pause in her walk to get around them.

Why did people stop in the middle of places, like an aisle at the grocery or a narrow path on the way to the falls, like now, to have a whole clump reunion? She didn't understand anything about clumps.

"Excuse me." The woman that was taking up most of the left side of the path just stared at her as she continued talking to the other female clump—there were children with her, so Sunny decided to call them clump-its. "I'd like to go through. Please?"

The Crusty Clump huffed at her. "Don't you see that we're having a private conversation here? You'll just have to figure out a different way to get around us. It's considered rude to interrupt someone when they're speaking. I'm surprised no one has told you that before." Sunny assured her they had, but she was just like that to not listen. "It figures. Just wait in line like the rest of the people here."

"No. You're the rude one. You have like fifty people in the line behind the clump you've created waiting to either come down or go up. Your clump is blocking a narrow path. I'd like to suggest—and right now, since I've finally graduated from anger management classes, I'm only suggesting this — that you get your flabby fat ass out of the way and have your 'private' conversations elsewhere. Though how you figure that with hundreds of people clambering around you to get through, you could have a private shit right now is beyond me. Everyone can hear every word you moo. But that's just me."

Sunny looked away to reign in her temper before it got the better of her. She didn't mind people around her hearing her talk to the women. Nor did she lie to her about the anger management classes. She knew she had temper and anger issues. But —

Sunny felt the pain in her shoulder just before she fell backwards and hit her head on one of the large stones that made up the Smokie Mountains. Christ, that had fucking hurt.

"You hit me." Crusty Clump nodded and used her cane like a sword, like she was parlaying or something. The warmth of what she thought might be blood slid down her back and into her eyes, so she couldn't see well. "You fucking hit me with that cane? Are you out of your ever-loving mind?"

"You're a rude young woman, and it doesn't surprise me at all that you've been to anger classes." Sunny tried to stand but was suddenly weak, her head spinning. "You stay right where you are, or so help me, I'll toss you over this mountainside, and they'll never find your body. Now. I'm going to finish my—" Sunny tried to get up and failed, hitting her head again. "Did I not just tell you to stay there? I'll hit you again, harder this time if you don't—"

Sunny didn't hear anymore over the roaring in her head. Her belly, usually all right with anything she shoved into her pie hole, was rebelling as well. Holding onto what she hoped was a tree, she nearly went over the side of the mountain when she heard a voice. Well, several of them, but the one that was closest to her was making the most sense.

"I'm going to put you down on the ground, all right?" Nodding was out of the question, and she wasn't sure any longer that she could make her mouth work. But the man seemed to understand. "My brother and I are going to carry you down the path, miss. Are you alone?"

"Crusty Clump hit me with her sword. My head hurts." He smiled, but she couldn't understand why her demise was funny to him. "No, I'm alone. No one likes to hang out with me. I'm sort of caustic. I'm a lot caustic." She grabbed her stomach. "I think I'm going to be sick."

She was too. Throwing up three times, the man held her hair out of the way. While she didn't know a great many things at the moment, she knew she'd had her hair in a ponytail when she left her hotel room that morning. Then Sunny tried to think why that was important. Laying her head back on the cooler rock, she closed her eyes.

"I'm going to need you to stay awake, miss. You more than likely have a concussion." She told him her first name. "All right, Sunshine—did your parents name you that because of your sunny disposition?"

"I'm sure they thought that was going to work, but I rebelled." Her eyes wouldn't focus. She saw three, or was it four of him right now? "Do you think you can stop fucking moving right now?" He told her they were going to pick her up. "I don't know if that's such a good idea. I'm seriously only just barely hanging on right—what the hell did you say again? Oh yes. Pain medication. Yes, that helps. I need to finish my walk today. Have the clumps of people moved yet?"

If he answered her again, she didn't know. The sudden feeling of being airborne hit her, and she was sick again. However, there was nothing left on her belly. Being picked up was too much. She begged them to toss her over the side and let gravity take her down. Sunny was sure it would have been a great deal less painful once she hit her head again.

Sunny was in and out of consciousness. Each time they had to stop, she was gagging. Not sure if she was telling them to stop or if they were that good, she was at the bottom of the hill before she could think where her bike was. If she could even find it, she told herself.

"I'll have someone look for it for you and make sure it's safe. Can you tell me what kind it is? Or the license plate number?" After telling him it was a Harley and that it was an Ohio plate, she slipped away. Another pinch to her arm told her she was getting more meds.

The ambulance ride was a series of questions shot at her, and to her, for the most part, her not answering them. She would have, but her mouth wasn't working again. The man who had brought her down the hill, she'd been told, was going to find her bike for her and put it away. The medic even told her how he'd gotten her down the hill.

"He and his brother carried you. The two of them are park rangers. Someone called the visitors center, and Gibb and Barron were the closest. They're good men—all the Cross men are." All clumps weren't that good. The man laughed, and she wondered again if she was talking aloud or if this man could read her mind. Before she could figure that one out, he started talking again. This time not to her.

Sunny was in the hospital, in a very bright room, when she opened her eyes. They were sorely mistaken if they had expected her to fight the meds they were giving her and stay awake. The man standing over her in a white lab coat asked her if she had any allergies. Sunny pointed to the band around her arm. Everything was listed there.

Waking again, she thought this was just getting stupid—she was able to talk. However, the feet, all she could see from her position, asked her to please lie still. He was stitching her up.

"I hit my head. That clump—person hit me with a cane or something." He said he'd been told that, but he was only there to make sure her head was stitched up. "I have a body cam. I'm required to wear it when I'm out because I have issues with clumps—uh, people."

"What do you call them? People?" She told him. "Clumps is a good name. Especially when they're clumped together like they do at times. Crazy Clump, the one that hit you, is a braying jackass if you ask me. She's telling everyone at the station house that you hit her first. I'm telling you that because we saw the body cam when you came in. The rangers are having a look at it." She asked him why. "Like I said, she's saying you hurt her first, and she had to defend herself. You have a wound on your shoulder,

Miss Meadow. They've decided not to stitch it just yet until the X-rays come back. Your collarbone is broken, and you have a concussion to the back of your head. When I'm finished here, they'll take you back to X-ray to get a few more pictures of your head. All right?"

She had so many people she needed to contact right now that she couldn't think where to start. When asked, she was given a little bit for the pain, and it took the edge off enough that when she looked down, the feet there had her remembering that a ranger had brought her down the hill. The boots, army issue, were dirty and used. Just the way she'd expect them to be.

"My name is Ranger Mark Cross. I'm not going to take your statement right now, Miss Meadow, but I would ask that if you think of something important, you relay it to me at once. Mrs. Hardgrave has been—" She asked him who that was. "Gibb said you called her Crusty Clump. She's in jail for assault. I'm assuming you will want to press charges."

"Yes. Please." She thought about the people

she had to contact. "I'm going to need a cell phone soon. I'm not just here for pleasure, though I'd stay if I could. This place is beautiful. I'm working, and I can't not check in."

"Officer Anderson was notified as soon as your name was put into the system as a search for next of kin." She thanked him. "No need for that. You must be pretty important if they contacted him not ten seconds after he spelled your name in the search line."

"No, not so much." She didn't tell him more but thought he'd never pass it on if she did. Sunny had no idea how she knew that, but she did. "I'm not human. I mean, mostly I am, but I'm not really."

"Elite shifter. I got that when they asked us to go to your aid. I suppose shifting would have taken care of your wounds, but we need it for court since you said you were pressing charges. I could smell it on you." She said that while she was an elite shifter, she didn't heal like others did. "I'm sorry for that. It's come in handy a few times over my life. Is there anything I can do for you?"

"Just my bike, which I was told is being taken care of." He told her that his brother Gibb was taking it to his house. "Okay. Then when can I get out of here? The sooner, the better."

"I can give you a cell phone to use. Yours, unfortunately, was broken when you were knocked back on your bottom. But as for leaving, since you can't heal, they'll need to keep you a few days. As I said, you can use a cell for your calls, but you have about two hundred stitches in your head alone." She asked him if he'd said two hundred. "Yes, I did. You hit your head once the first time, but when you tried to get up, you fell back twice more, and from what we can ascertain from your body cam, you hit your head three more times. There was a sharp protrusion there, and you managed to hit it each time you fell back."

"Christ." He chuckled a little and told her that was the way he reacted. "I'm going to take you up on your offer of the phone, Ranger. I do have to check in once a day with my boss, or I'm toast."

"I've spoken to him." When his feet disappeared,

she heard the door close to wherever they were. "I was told to make sure you had all the help you needed, including a gun, should you not have one on you at all times. I was also told to make sure you knew he has watched the recording of your morning and isn't concerned with that at the moment. He did tell me you're not just caustic, as you told my brother, but you're a pain in the ass as well. Mr. Rugby told me you were here to find an escaped prisoner. And that if anyone could bring her in, it would be you. You're related to her."

"She's my sister-in-law. So I guess I'm technically related to her, but thank goodness I'm not blood-related. She killed four men in Ohio and has killed one more on the way here that I know of. The reason I'm telling you this is nothing I can figure out. I keep my mouth shut like a virgin at a Friday night football game keeps her legs closed." Mark laughed, and she smiled. "The only thing I ask of you, Mark, is to stay the hell out of my way. She's fucking dangerous and won't hesitate to kill whatever or whoever gets in her way."

"Your brother and sister." She didn't answer but was surprised David had told him so much. "I'll help you in any way I can. My entire family works here in this park, so we can keep our ears and noses open for you. We're all bears, black bears, who live on the mountain. Also, I was told to tell you that if you get hurt again, David was going to kick your ass and bury you in the backyard of his home. He said he knows you'll believe him too."

"You know, he only uses that tone with me. I don't know what it is that I've ever done to him to warrant such threats, but he does it time and time again." The man laughed again. "I've been on disciplinary leave for a month now. I'm, as you said, caustic to work with. However, once the big shits got their heads out of their asses and looked at the tape, I was released from it. I liked the class, however, so I finished the course. It's all in the way you think rather than the way you react. I usually react first, feel really good about it, then get into trouble. And if you ask me if I ever feel any remorse for what I do, I'll tell you what I told the shrink. No fucking way."

Mark was still laughing when she heard the door open again. "Miss Meadow, we're going to take you to surgery in a few moments. The doctor will be in to see you soon."

Panic took her breath away. She didn't want to be put under. Didn't want to feel like she wasn't going to be able to handle herself when she was out. The meds she'd taken earlier had been just for the pain, and her lack of sleep had put her under. But with surgery, she'd be deep under and—

"Sunny, take a breath." She heard the voice of Mark but couldn't focus well on it. "Sunny, I'm going to hit you to make you breathe if you don't do it soon. You're scaring the nice nurse here, and she is going to be sick. Breathe right now."

The compulsion of his order had her breathing again. His face, a nice handsome one, appeared in front of her. He was laying his head on the floor and looking up at her. His smile and charm had her thinking this man thought he was all that and a bag of chips, but she knew handsome men like him. All bark and no talk.

"Breathe in and out. All right. I'm talking to you this way because you can't be rolled to your back just yet. Are you still with me?" She said she was. "All right. When you were hit with the cane, not a sword, Cranky Clump broke your collar bone, and there are several chips of bone in your muscle. They're going to repair your shoulder without using any kind of screws or such and take out the small pieces. The small pieces are going to be put back on the broken bone with some kind of stitching, so you'll be able to shift when you need to. So far, so good, right?"

"Yes. Are you making fun of me?" He said his wife would have his head if he tried that shit. "You're very charming. I didn't want to be caught up in your bullshit, but it sounds like someone has your ass. Too bad, I was thinking about how handsome you are."

"Maybe we'll be related in some way. I have five brothers. You've only met three of them so far, so our chances of—"

"Nope, and no fucking way, no. I don't want a mate or a husband, or even a wife if that's the way things go. I got enough shit going on in my corner to last about fifty lifetimes. No thanks. Keep them away, and we'll call it even on you having my back." He said he didn't think that was going to be possible. "Make it possible, or I'll hurt you. Believe me when I tell you, neither you nor your bear will come out on top if you try something."

"I believe you." He didn't move while they put an IV in her arm for the surgery. "They're going to take you up to the second floor right now, and you'll be in a room with others until your surgery is finished. After you're okay to leave recovery, they'll send you on to your room. I'll be there waiting for you. I'll have you a gun for when you're able to take it as well."

"Thank you. I'm better now." He still didn't move, and she felt bad that he had to lay on the floor. "Get up, you moron, before I spit on you, and it lands in your mouth. Go on. I have shit to do, and you're not going to get any brownie points for laying around."

She was moved into an elevator while he was still laughing. He did ride up to the third floor with her and even told her good luck when she was taken beyond where he could go. Christ, what a waste of a nice man. She certainly hoped his wife knew the kind of man she was married to. Ten minutes after arriving on the surgical floor, she was wheeled into a bright white room and put under. Her panic didn't seem to be as bad this time.

~*~

Mark was still in the waiting room when Jamie contacted him. She'd been working on her last job for the agency, and he was thrilled for her. She told him she was going home, having a nice nap in the sunshine.

Be careful, honey. It's supposed to thunderstorm soon, and I'd hate for you to be caught up in it. She told him that he was a party pooper. *I am at that. I have to tell you about this woman I'm babysitting right now. She's the kind of woman you only read about and wish you could just simply say the things that she does at a moment's notice.*

He told her everything that had happened since she'd been picked up. Nothing about her being here to find her sister-in-law, but everything else. When she laughed with him about her calling people clumps, he told her he loved her.

And I love you. I'd like to meet her. Or do you think she's only talking this way because of the pain? Mark assured her she was the real deal. *Good. I hope she's one of your brothers' mates. Not that any one of them could handle a — what did you call her?*

Caustic. And I was thinking the same thing. She needs to have someone strong enough to put up with her daily. Jamie agreed with him. *I have to stay with her. Not only is she here on business, but she is a little higher on the food chain than I am. I don't know what she does for a living, nor what branch, if any, she might work with, but I've been assigned to make sure she has what she needs when she needs it.* Gibb said she was not one to hold back when she had something to say.

At least you'll be able to have a little fun with her. Not too much, but just enough. Oh, before I forget, Bobby's family arrived today. They're a nice couple of people. I think they're a little shocked by him and his sisters being around. They'd not even been told there had been a marriage or kids from it. I'm glad someone is going to be taking care of them. He said he was too. *Also, I heard from the prison where Williams is. He's in solitary confinement and still causing trouble. The thing is, he's bragging that it took anyone so long to find him. Some people are just nuts, I guess. We should have him locked in a cell with Sunny. I'm betting she can take care of his ass for us.*

I'm betting she'd come out on top even if he was armed.

They talked for a little while longer, and she told him she really needed a nap. He didn't blame her for that. Mark had been keeping her up most nights making love, and she'd gotten up early this morning and gone out to California to do a hunt for a cadaver. Then on top of all that, Molly, her oldest dog, had died in her sleep.

She'd been about fourteen years old. It had broken her heart bad enough that he'd had to hold her all night. Not that it was a hardship for him to hold her, but he had hurt for her. The other two took it hard as well. Sidekick, the youngest, hadn't left Jamie's side the entire night.

He didn't know what she'd found when she was called out. Rarely did she tell him anything about the bodies she was looking for. But he did know she was looking for a missing person from about six years ago. The family wanted to cash in the insurance policy that had been on hold, and the company wanted to make sure the woman was indeed dead. He'd have to find out from her what she'd found out.

Stretching out his legs, he was happy when Dexter joined him with not just a few bottles of water but some dinner as well. They said the surgery would be about four hours—to him, that seemed a long time—but that recovery would be about the same time. Eating his sandwich, Dexter told him what he'd been able to find out about the owl he'd been sent to see.

"He was hurt, just like the camper said. However, I have a feeling he wasn't hurt until the camper saw him. Poor thing looked like he'd gone from sitting up in a nice perch to being tossed around in the dryer for a load or two. I've sent him on to the vet, but I don't hold out much hope of him getting better." That sucked, too, Mark told him. "Yes, I think so too. But without proof, whoever hurt him is going to get away with it. Tomorrow morning I'm going to see if I can find his home. I don't know if he might have a mate around, but if he and his mate are sitting on some chicks, she's going to need some help with them. At least until another mate comes along."

"If you need some help, ask Jamie's dad to go with you. He's becoming quite the outdoorsman. Last night I saw that he was looking through some of my old books and reading up on the park. He would enjoy that, I believe." Dexter said he'd give him a call. "Grannie told me he's doing well at work. She thinks he's a funny man by the way he doesn't raise his voice when he's making a point. I like hanging around with him too."

"Yeah, and his daughter isn't so bad either. Right?" He laughed and said he loved her. "Well, duh, you moron. Of course, you do. I have to get going. I have about fifty things to do before I can get to bed. Laundry, for one thing, and packing me something to eat on the trail tomorrow. I hate taking just a bunch of those nature bars. Yuck."

After he left him, Mark pulled out his phone and played a few games of solitaire. He'd rather play the real thing, but the phone kept him entertained in a pinch. When the nurse came to tell him that Sunny was in recovery, he thanked her and called her boss. He had a feeling this was the man's personal cell phone number, as he only answered it with "Hello." He told him what he knew, which wasn't much.

"She'll be in recovery for four hours or so, they told me. Once she's finished there, she'll be moved to a room." He said he was sending guards to decorate—not to guard, but to decorate—her door. "I don't know what she does for you. Or what you do, for that matter. Should I be concerned?"

"Not so long as you keep your head about you and don't piss her off." He said he had a feeling she was easily pissed off. "She is at that. However, when she's pissy, and you don't deserve it, she'll apologize to you. But that doesn't happen often. Just keep her safe while she's there alone. I'm sending you a picture of her sister-in-law so you can know who to look for. Show it to whoever you trust. The woman is dangerous. Armed or not, she can kill without hesitation."

"Which one? I'm thinking you're talking about the sister-in-law, but I also think that could pertain to Sunny too." The man laughed and said that was right. "I'm going to remain in the dark until something happens, aren't I?"

"Yes. It'll be safer for you if you are until such time as I get something back on you and your family that tells me otherwise." Mark figured as much but didn't say anything. "I will tell you this one thing, and you're to take it to your grave—Sunny isn't a typical anything. Not woman, shifter, or someone that works for me. She's more than just a little special, and I want you to treat her like she's a national treasure. Don't coddle her or try to change her mind. If she tells you something, you can consider it gospel. You'll die if you don't. And that is from me."

Even after talking to her boss, Mark didn't know what was going on. But as the man had indicated, it was really none of his business unless she got hurt.

He was really glad he'd not blamed him for her being hurt this time. However, now that he thought about it, he wondered what was going to happen to the clumps that had hurt her. Only time would tell, he supposed.

Chapter 1

Needing to move was making her legs ache, and her body feel like it was drenched in lead. Yesterday Sunny had been in recovery, and today she was in her room. The surgery had been to repair her collarbone that had been shattered as well as stitches in her head. A clump person had beaten her with her cane when she'd asked her to take her conversation off the path to the top of the mountain. She'd beaten her badly enough that she'd needed over two hundred stitches in her head and back.

So since she wasn't a regular person to the Smokie Mountain Park, she'd been given a full guard watching over her. There were two guards around her at all times, with two more at her door. She'd bet too that there were other staff members that were part of the crew that David, her boss, had sent to watch over her.

Sunny was on an assignment when she came to the Great Smokie Mountains. However, she'd just been out walking when she'd been hurt. Well, she was not just walking but trying her best to burn off some of the energy she was forever combating. If she wasn't able to do that, then she got more caustic than she normally was. And boy, oh boy, Sunny could be caustic when the mood suited her.

David Rugby had been her boss since she'd been first recruited into service eight years ago. There were days that she regretted his coming to find her on base, but other days she thought him to be all right. Sunny didn't like people as a whole and hated when they were all together worse.

A single person, she'd always heard, was nice. Could even be called generous. But when there was a group of them, a clump she called them all the time, they were worse than a toddler without a nap.

Christ, she hated people more than she did herself at times.

"Agent Meadows?" She didn't bother looking at the person at the door when he spoke. "My name is Dexter Cross. My older brother, Mark, sent me here to give you a gun as well as a badge that came in the mail for you. Well, I don't suppose one would call a helicopter landing in the middle of an open field with guns pointed at us as mail, but then I guess it was needed, and the field was—"

"What the fuck? Do you babble all the time? Christ, just hand it over and then get the fuck out of here. I've got more important things to do rather than to listen to you empty your fucking head." He grinned at her. "You're not cute if that's what you're going for. Your brother, at least he could be charming when it suited—why the fuck are you still standing over there? Are you expecting me to get out of his mother fucking bed and take it from you?"

"No." He laughed and started moving toward her. "You're as nasty as I was told you were." Sunny didn't bother correcting him on his assumption that she was nasty. It was her trademark. But she did put out her hand to him. "I'm to tell you before I hand it over that I'm a federal officer, same as you. Not as decorated but the same. If you shoot me, there is going to be a great deal of paperwork to fill out, and David said he'd not be happy with your ass."

Sunny narrowed her eyes at him. "Hand the weapon over before I get really nasty with you and leap out of this fucking bed and tear out your throat." When he stiffened and handed the gun to her without a word, she made sure that there was a full clip on the Glock, then racked one into the chamber. "What is it?"

Her whispered question had him moving toward the bed where she was. However, he never turned his back to the door once he had turned to look at it. Just as she was ready to demand for him to get his head out of his ass and answer her, she smelled the blood too.

"Don't get in my way." He said he'd not get in her way that she was his mate. It took her a full minute to understand what he'd said. But he didn't turn to look at her, nor did he say anything more about her being his mate. Since there were more important things going on right now, she pushed it to the back of her mind for now. Then she was going to kill the man beside her.

"There were four guards outside of your door when I entered. They checked my badge and then called it in. The older of the four, he told me it was shift change." She didn't tell him to tell her what he'd seen and was happy that he'd known enough to tell her. "I've contacted my brothers. All of them are on their way here. Do you see the blood under the door?"

"Yes. I do now." She wasn't sure what to do. A first in her line of work. Just as she was going to tell him to go into the bathroom, to stay out of her way, he simply disappeared and in his place was a huge fucking black bear. "Now, what the fuck am I supposed to do to keep you safe? Ever think of that before you shifted into something larger than this fucking little assed room?"

He nipped at her leg after licking it. She didn't

want to be pissed off at that but didn't want him to get it into his head that she was okay with it, either. Just as she was going to slide out of the bed, the door flew open. Sunny didn't even have time to fire before the bear—she supposed it was Dexter was out the door and on top of whatever had been on the other side.

Sunny wanted to get up, but she was suddenly down on the floor with one of the brothers. She knew that he had to be related to Mark and the lummox that was out in the hall. They all smelled the same—like comfort. Though she'd never, in a million years, say that out loud to them.

It took them too fucking long, as far as she was concerned, for anyone to tell her what the hell was going on. Instead of having someone come into the room and talk to her, she was getting her information in bits and pieces as the men in the room talked around her. Finally having enough, she pulled out her weapon and pointed it at the head of the man sitting on the bed next to her. He laughed rather than being upset with her.

"I want answers." He told her that he could see that. "Well? What the fuck are you waiting on? Tell me what the hell is going on and who out there was killed. Because as surely as I'm sitting here, for all the manpower here, there had better be a dead body someplace."

"There are six dead bodies out in the hallway." She felt horrible for saying that. And she was reasonably sure that, she thought his name was Gibb, had meant for her to feel that way. "Two nurses are dead. And all four of the men sent here to protect you. They were shot in the head from another room. My brothers are out looking for the shooter now. I'm to stay here with you as my brother—just so you know, I'm not happy with this assignment, but my brother Dexter said you were his mate, and I was to protect you with my life."

"You're not happy with me or the fact that you have to babysit me?" He looked like he was thinking on it when he finally told her both. "I guess that I'd not be happy with that assignment letter. However, do you happen to know if dumbass is all right? He should have waited for me to—" She didn't know what she wanted to have him wait for, now that she thought about it.

"To what? Get hurt? Or wait until you were dead before he reacted? No matter how badass you are, which I'm assuming that you're very much so, he would never let you get hurt if it came down to you or him. Dexter gravely wounded one of the men that had been drawing on you, by the way." She was hurting because the man, Gibb, she thought again, was being so calm about telling her that she'd been stupid. Not in those words, but she did feel it all the same. "Dexter told me to be nice to you. He can feel my anger. So, I'm sorry."

"No, you're not. And I don't want you to say things to me unless you mean it. Are you sorry that you spoke to me like you did?" He shook his head. "Good. I would have to tell you that I'm sorry then. And so you know, I hate admitting that, but I was a bitch, and I took it out on you. However, that doesn't mean that I won't snap again. I tend to get bitchier the longer I feel like I'm in the dark about shit going on around me. Or, for that matter, things going on to me. What the fuck is going on right now, Gibb?"

"Straight up? I can handle that. But don't ask me something unless you want the truth from now on. All of it." She nodded. "Dexter was shot. Once in the belly, but he's going to be just fine once he shifts. He and my brothers Mark and Frazier are out looking for the person who killed the four guards and the nurses. The man that shot Dexter smells like the room where the shooter was standing. So that's all they have to go on just now."

"Was it a woman that was the shooter?" He said that it was. "How did Dexter know to kill the man, which I'm only assuming right now was drawing a bead on me?"

"He's not dead but not talking either. The Feds took him as soon as they arrived." She nodded.

"How were the others killed? You said shot, but I've got a feeling that the nurses didn't get that quick death."

"No. They were both tortured. Terribly. Nurse Mable had her skin peeled away from her face before she was stabbed in the heart. The other nurse, Nurse Joey, was killed by his bleeding out. The killer cut off his fingers one at a time and then went for his wrist. I don't know, but I have a feeling that she'd not meant for it to go so quickly. But Joey was on blood thinners, and he bled out faster than normal." For some reason, it hurt her again that someone's life had been taken so that they could get to her. "I have a picture if you'd like to see what the woman looked like." She nodded. "Mark said he didn't want to bother you with it as so many had been killed when Diane came for you. But Dexter said to tell you because you wouldn't be prepared for her if you didn't know she was this close."

"He's right. I can't fight what I don't know." He handed her the picture, and she handed it back to him. "Yes, that's Diana. She knows where I am and that I'm hurt. That won't bode well for anyone in this town."

"That's what Dexter just told me. There are two more bodies with her MO on them as well. They're being attached to this homicide." She nodded.

"Dexter said he's on his way back to talk to you. He isn't hurt anymore, but he is upset. I'm sure that you can feel his anger."

"I can now that you mention it." She laid back on the bed after having help from Gibb to get up from the floor. "I'm not happy with him, either. He could have been killed running out in the hall when those people were out there with guns."

"I was using the element of surprised on them." Dexter came into the room and looked at his brother. "Thanks. I owe you for this. Mark and the others are at the crime scene and need your help."

As soon as they were alone, she stood up again and slapped him across the face. Drawing back to hit him again, he grabbed her wrist to stop her, and he asked her if she'd tell him what he'd done to deserve that.

"You could have been killed." He told her again that he was using the fact that they'd forget they were armed. "So you ran out there hoping they'd forget that they were armed and run off? That's the stupidest thing I've ever heard."

"It worked." She glared at him and crossed her arms over her chest in defiance. "But it did work. I've done this before, love. I promise you that I didn't go into this without some thought as to what might have happened. My only concern was to take out the person that was set to kill you. However, I do have a question. Why would she want you dead? I could feel her anger toward you. What is it that makes this sister-in-law, no blood relation to you, want you dead so desperately?"

"Because of all the people in the world, I can find her. So in finding her, I take away her fun. Diana kills for no other reason than she enjoys it. She's a sadist." He asked her why she could find her when no others could, not that he didn't believe her. "I have this knack that…it's hard to explain. I can search for people and have a sort of tag with them. I'm not explaining that very well. Say, I find your brother, Mark. He's at this moment sitting in a car talking to your other brother Barron. They're discussing the people killed in the hospital. And how they were killed."

"What if I told you that I can feel the same thing? That not only can I hear what they're saying, but I can also see them sitting in Mark's truck in front of the office where they both work when I concentrate." She nodded. "You figured this would happen when you found your mate."

"No. I didn't think I'd ever find my mate. It just didn't seem to be in the cards for me." He kissed her and then smiled. "I'm not sure what you were thinking when you did that, but I would like to know why you kissed me."

"You're beautiful, and I belong to you. I've also fallen in love with you." She cocked her head at him, and he smiled. "You don't believe me? I can't lie to you. Not that I would, but I can't anyway. I do love you. Very much so. And like you, I didn't know that there might be someone out there that would take pity on me and take me into their heart." She snorted at him.

"You're very funny. A good-looking man like you? I'm sure you've had a great deal of sex in your lifetime." He told her none that mattered as much as it would be to make love to her when she was ready. "I don't know if I'm ready or not. I've got so much going on in my head right now that I'm not sure what I feel towards you."

"Understandable. But I want you to know that I'm here for you. Not just for sex but for whatever you need from me." When the door flew open behind them, he shoved her behind him, and she could feel his bear. He relaxed a little when they saw that it was only his brother Frazier but not by much.

"We're going to get her out of here now." Without a word, she shifted her body into a small mouse and told Dexter to put her in his pocket. "I...I'm glad you thought of that. Christ, the things we've been talking about in a way to get you moved out of here undetected. All right, let's go."

Once she was in Dexter's pocket, she felt safer than she had in a long while. Not knowing where they were going nor what was going on didn't bother her as much as she thought it should have.

~*~

Diana was bored. Even watching the man

bleed out didn't do anything for her. Standing up as he begged for his life, she pointed her gun at him and ended his noise. Christ, didn't people understand that begging was just annoying? Anyway, she made her way to the barn door where she'd been staying and looked out over the mountains beyond where she was.

"This place is a killer's dream." It was too. There were so many cubby holes in the mountains that she could carry on her business, and no one would find the body for decades. That was something that few understood. She didn't care to be famous or even have her name in the paper. She just liked to kill.

It had taken her nearly a month to shake the tail that she'd had on her when she'd left Canada. It had been both fun and annoying to have people chasing after her. Diana had been hiding out there, having some fun after she'd killed Basil and Daffodil, her husband and his sister. They should have been thrilled to be dead after having to go through life with names like they had. If their parents weren't already dead, she might well have killed them too.

Idiots.

Then there was Sunny. Sunshine Lily Meadows.

Christ, she hated that woman. Each and every time she turned a corner, there she was. It should have made her feel good that she'd yet to take her in, but it did curtail her fun to have to be constantly looking over her shoulder to see if that bitch was coming for her.

And she had been too. With each and every kill, Diana had barely gotten out before there she was. Like in the hospital. Diana knew that a part of her nearly being caught was her own fault. Hanging around to kill off as many people as she could had been her downfall. But it seemed to her that it was a good opportunity nearly missed if she were to have just walked away from such an easy, fun time. Then there was the bear.

It wasn't as if she didn't know there were shifters. Her own husband had been one. It was the only reason that she had married the fool. To get herself a baby that she could train to be her partner in her fun. It boggled her mind when she'd been thinking about all the things that could be handed to her on a silver platter with having an elite shifter at her disposal. But it wasn't to be. Basil couldn't sire children with her.

"Not that it had anything to do with my age." She grinned when she thought of what the doctor had told her that faithful afternoon she'd gone to see him with Basil. She had wanted it to be his fault, but the doctor had figured out that she was much older than she had professed and having pointed out her age to her was what had gotten him killed. Along with Basil, the doctor's nurse, the people in the waiting room, as well as the people on the elevator that she'd had to use. Then she'd killed Daffodil, who had been waiting in the car for them to return just because she could.

Had she had a moment or two to think about it, she might well not have killed Basil or his sister. Simply because doing so brought Sunny to her, and that was something that she'd not counted on. Honestly, she'd never given the other woman a single thought before then.

Diana knew that Sunny worked for some kind of government office. What she did wasn't anything she'd thought to check into before then. After talking to her a couple of times, she thought her too stupid to be much more than a plaything for some office jerk or even a woman that delivered mail. But she'd been so much more. Thinking on the conversation she'd had with her just after she moved to Canada, she had been afraid for the first time in her life. And all because of a woman named Sunshine of all things.

"You killed my family." She hadn't any idea what was going on when a voice suddenly started talking to her in her head. "You killed a lot of people, but I'm coming for you now, and there will be no stopping me once I get to you, Diana. Killing my brother was bad enough, but Daff was only sixteen when you murdered her, and for that, I'm going to make you pay."

"Sunshine? Christ, how come I'm only finding out this kind of shit after I'm no longer married to your brother? He should have been more forthcoming. Don't you think?" She didn't answer her. "Never mind. Basil didn't have anything I wanted after I was told that I couldn't have any kids by him. Can you imagine the kind of kids I would have been able to train to be like me? It would have been epic."

"You killed him because you were too old to have a child with him. I don't think that's even remotely his fault." Diana didn't like being reminded of her age, and Sunny had thought it was funny. "I never thought you were as young as you said you were. In fact, even the doctor had it wrong that you were only in your late forties. You're closer to fifty-five, aren't you, Diana?"

"Fuck you." The laughter rang through her ears for hours after she stopped speaking to Sunny. But that was only the beginning for the two of them to be talking all the time. Every time that she was close to having some fun, there she'd be. Telling her not just where she was but the name of the person she was killing. Right up until she found out that Sunny had had her head banged in, and the talking stopped. The nudge to her mind had her thinking that she was well enough to talk to her again.

"*It's not over, you know.*" Diana looked around for her sister-in-law and was shocked that she'd so easily contacted her. "*You'll be dismayed to find out too that I'm much stronger than I was before, Diana. Not only that, but I can see exactly where you are right at this moment in longitude and latitude too. You're going to be dead before the next time you kill. This I will guarantee you.*"

Diana looked up at the sky when she heard a chopper go by. When all it did was hover over where she was, it took her a moment to realize that someone from it was shooting at her. As soon as the bullet that entered her arm stopped burning, Diana found herself running down the mountain she had been on and looking for a place to hide. Christ, how in the hell did they do that without her knowing they were coming up on her?

"*As I said, I'm stronger than before. And I'm thinking that I'll only get stronger from here. You can no longer hide from me, Diana. I'll have you dead before too much longer, and once you are, then the world will be a better place than it has ever been before.*" She heard the dogs barking, and their noise was getting closer all the time. *"Those would be Roxy and Sidekick. My newest family members' cadaver dogs. They'll hunt for living people too, but since I know you're going to be dead soon enough, they're looking for you now."*

She was running as fast as she could. *"Shut the fuck up."* Diana fell twice on her way down the hill and nearly broke her arm when it got tangled up in some kind of underbrush. It had startled her, too, when creatures seemed to be chasing her down the hill as well. A fox and a lion, of all things, were right on her tail too. *"What do you have, some kind of zoo after me? Christ, why don't you leave me the fuck alone, and I'll do the same for you?"*

"Not going to happen, I'm afraid. The cougar, not a lion, is Richard. He told me that you're banged all up so badly that he thinks too that you might have shit on your face." She reached up to check if she did when she stopped sliding and pulled away what did look like shit. Rubbing it on the weeds beside her, she heard laughter again. *"That was poison ivy, Diana. I'm afraid you're going to be a mess when the police get to you."*

Standing up, she took off running again, only to end up sliding more down the hill. Christ, she hurt in places she had never felt before, and it wasn't until she realized that there was nothing coming up in front of her that she should have been paying more attention to her surroundings. As soon as she was airborne, the water below her seemed to suck her right into it.

It took her all of three seconds to get over the good feeling of being clean. Then the rocks started to pound into her from every direction. Her head, arms and legs seemed to be taking the brunt of it. Even her fingers seemed to be breaking to pieces as she was tossed around like she'd been put into a washing machine.

Reaching for anything and everything that she could touch only made the water toss her around more. Long logs would hold her up for a few minutes only to be shoved aside, and she'd go tumbling again. There was no way she was going to survive this if she didn't get out of the water soon.

When she saw land close enough to her to

maybe swim to, Diana dragged her broken body to the edge as best she could. It didn't work out the way that she had hoped it would, and she ended up further down the waterway than she had hoped. The land was getting further away from her, and she knew too that her wrist was broken as well as her ankle. There wasn't any way that she was going to be walking away from this anytime too soon.

Getting onto the embankment that she was nearest, Diana puked for a good ten minutes before she felt like she'd emptied all the nasty water from her stomach. Even laying on the rocky shoreline was more comfortable than she had thought it should have been.

"You're about ten minutes from being caught, Diana. Any last words before you're taken in? Perhaps you can tell me something profound? I don't know, maybe tell me that you're sorry." The dogs were closer now, and she just laid there, not even bothering to answer Sunny. *"That's really too bad for you. By the way, you might like to know too that you're not going to stand trial but go straight to prison for the rest of your life."*

"Fuck you and the horse you rode in on." That had seemed more of a threat when it was in her head. *"You'll be with the dogs, I'm assuming? What are you going to do when I kill them too? Nothing. You can't do shit to me because I know you're related to me."*

"We're not related by blood, moron. Christ, when I think of all the times I tried to warn Basil away from you, I want to kick my own ass because I didn't try harder to get you out of our lives. I know I'd still be looking for you, but you'd not have killed off my brother and sister." Diana just laughed and looked up at the dog standing over her. *"I see the troops have arrived. And in answer to your question, yes, I am with them."*

There was a medical team with the dogs that Diana was so happy to see. Once she was given some pain medication — she was sure they only gave her the minimum amount — Diana was put on a gurney that wasn't the least bit comfortable and then attached to a large rope.

No one spoke to her as they waited around for whatever was coming for her. Sunny didn't speak to her either, for which she was grateful. The pain was really making her want to scream, but she had no intentions of making a scene with her around. While she enjoyed begging from her victims, she wasn't going to stoop so low as to beg from Sunny.

Her rights weren't read to her. Not that she would have understood them. She was hurting so badly now that they could have told her that she was going to be set free, and it would have made little difference to how she was feeling right now. When she was attached to something and shaken up a bit, Diana passed out. She was flying through the air when she woke the next time and screamed out in not just pain but a fear like she'd never felt before.

She knew that Sunny was going to have her dropped from the sky. A little bit of her would have actually welcomed it, she thought. When she saw the men on the helicopter pulling her into the place where they were, she did beg then. Not just for meds to knock her out, but she also begged them to drop her out of the helicopter to her death. It was something she never thought she'd wish for in her life. To not just die but to have it done so quickly.

Chapter 2

Dexter made his way along the path. The group with him was an older bunch of people, but they were fun to be with. He made sure that he took breaks when they began to look a little winded and answered their questions as they brought them up. Just as they were headed to the old homestead, he heard from his brother Ewing.

"They've taken Diana into custody just now. She's on her way to the hospital to have surgery. There are as many guards around her as I've ever seen before." He asked how Sunny was doing. *"I think she's doing all right. I guess you would know better than I would, but she holds her thoughts close to her chest, doesn't she? I*

thought for sure that she'd stomp on Diana when we came up on her, but all she did was watch the surroundings and commented once on how beautiful it was around where we were."

The thing was, he didn't know much about Sunny. He was in love with her, but with everything going on, they'd not had a great deal of time to just talk. Dexter didn't know any more about her than she did him. And that he supposed was his fault as he'd not really made a lot of time for her. Their jobs were getting in the way of everything right now.

"Are you off tomorrow?" Ewing said that he was. *"I was wondering if you'd trade with me. I have the office tomorrow, so it wouldn't be that bad. I could use some time down with Sunny. To get to know her and get our lives off to a better start than we're having right now."*

"Sure." Just like that, his brother was willing to do this for him, and Dexter was humbled by it. *"If you do me one favor. Please have us all over for dinner soon. Not tomorrow, but sometime in the future. We don't know her all that well either."*

"Deal." The rest of the afternoon was a great

deal better to do. He'd managed to see a hawk get his dinner and had been lucky enough to show the people he was with. Also, he enjoyed just knowing that tomorrow he was going to be spending some good time with Sunny. Even if they didn't make love, they'd at least be able to hang out together.

After the walk, he was headed back to the office for his next group when his cell phone rang. It wasn't something he carried after being off work, but since he had just given the number to Sunny that morning, he was glad to hear from her.

"I have a question. I know that's a stupid way to start a conversation, but I just thought of something. I have a house in DC that I need to get some things from." He said he just happened to have the day off tomorrow if she wanted to do it then. "Really? I thought that I'd have to beg or something. This is great. Also, I'd like to figure out a way for this area to be my permanent address. I love it here."

"I do as well. Before I forget to ask you too, Ewing wants us to have everyone over for dinner sometime. Not tomorrow, but soon so the others can get to know you." She said she'd like that too but didn't know him either. "That's the reason that I traded with him. So that we can hang out together and get some things sorted out with the house and us. Grannie is having dinner with us all on Sunday, our usual family get-together, but with us having the next three days off, I'm usually off on Thursday and Friday. We'll have three days to just be getting things done."

"I'd like that. Yeah, that sounds really good." He was glad too and asked her when she wanted to leave in the morning. "It won't take us long to get there. David is sending us a chopper to get us there and back. I do have some paperwork to fill out for my checks and shit to get paid with. Also, did you hear that Diana is being operated on right now? They want her healthy to go to prison. Dumbest thing I've ever heard, but then I'm not in charge of shit like that."

"Ewing told me. They want her healthy so that she can spend as much time as possible behind bars. I don't know about you, but I'm glad she will be paying the price for a long time." She said she supposed that was as good as she was going to get with her killing her only family. "I'm sorry about that. I truly am. However, I want you to know that you've been a part of our family since the day I met you. We all love you."

"And I love you all too. Your Grannie is a hoot, by the way. And she makes me want to be nice around her. I think she could hurt me too." They both laughed. "Also, I want to jump your bones soon."

"I can be where you are in about ten minutes." They both laughed. "I have to work until six tonight. I'm on tour duty today. Not that I don't mind that, but it's sort of boring when I can be out in the woods doing things more productive. Right now, I'm not sure what that would be, but it is better than sitting in an office all day. That's what I was going to be doing tomorrow. Ewing is taking over for me so I can have three days off together."

"I have some downtime for the next several weeks. I usually don't take it all when I'm finished with something. That's another thing we have to talk about. My job. David, you've met him. He wants to sit down with you to talk about what I do for the government as well. It's very hush hush." He knew she realized that they were both working for the Feds but in a different capacity. But what she did wasn't entirely clear to him. "Also, my pay. I did mention that I have to set that up with a local bank, but there is also the insurance that I have from my family when they were killed."

"We have, each of us has insurance money from when our parents were killed as well as other things that we've been doing since we were children. I've got a side business that I do as well as the rest of us. Grannie has a nice shop in town where we all have some of the things we make in them. I blow glass. It's what relaxes me when I'm super stressed."

"I can see where what you do can be stressful. Jamie was telling me about Mark having to put down three bears not long ago. That must have been hard for him. But the people that had been on his tour that day, she told me, were charged with their deaths. Under Federal law, they were responsible for their deaths as much as if they'd pulled the trigger themselves." He asked her if she knew anything about the trial for Hardgrave. "I'm going to only have to be there if there is a problem. I don't foresee anything coming up where I'd have to show, but I have to be available. It's starting on Monday. David is having her investigated so that things go better than they might well have done if she were only being tried in a regular court of law. Because of where she hit me and the fact that she hit me, means that she's going to be tried with things being a federal crime."

"I think I might have known that but didn't think about it. I've heard, too, that she's been complaining in the jail a great deal about nearly everything. The food isn't up to par. There is something wrong with her bed. The usual things that she wouldn't have to deal with had she not been such a bitch." He pulled up in front of the office to get his list and told Sunny where he was. "I have to go in and get things done so that I can finish up my day to be with you. I was thinking we should have dinner out someplace that's not a tourist place. I'll have Grannie find us someplace nice."

After hanging up, he went into the office to pick up his list. It was important to know how many people were going to be with him at any given time. That way, if they wandered away or, as it happened in most cases, decided to leave before the tour was finished, he could account for everyone he'd left with. It was a great deal like babysitting, he knew, but it was the way they'd been able to keep people safe for so long. As he was headed to the next meeting place, he knew there was going to be a bit of a delay. Elk had come out to graze in the open field, and people were stopping to see them.

Usually, one or more of them would come to the rescue of the people. Elk could be very territorial when it suited them, and they'd have to keep the people back out of their way. Today was one of those days. Not only that, but a few kids had decided that rules didn't apply to them for some reason and were within a few feet of the grazing herd when he came up to help out.

"Back off. Now." The older kid, Dexter thought

him to be in his mid to early twenties, just laughed at him. "Do you want to die, kid? They don't like to be disturbed while they're having lunch."

"They're just a bunch of deer with horns. We have them on our land all the time. Besides, you have a gun to use if they get too frisky." As the kid made his way toward the group of about twenty or so elk, some of them with their kids, he waited until the larger of the big animals noticed the group of kids before he moved. Keeping idiots safe was getting harder and harder all the time."

The bear came out of nowhere, and he knew it was one of his brothers. However, just as it ran the boy down, knocking him out of the way of the charging elk leader, Dexter was surprised to see that it was his grandda. The boy and his companions were screaming their heads off just as the charging herd was running in the opposite direction of his growling grandda. What he did next would be talked about for years, if not for centuries.

Grandda didn't suffer fools well. When he turned back to the teenagers and ran them down, he caught one of the kids by the shoe and knocked him down. Standing over him, his grandda, even for his age, stood up on his hind feet and roared. It was a magnificent site and one that Dexter wouldn't soon forget. Making his way to the kid, he yelled at his grandda as if he were a regular bear to move on. With a wink at him, he finally moved on but not before taking the kid's backpack with him as he ran to the woods. Dexter would get it back to the kid later if he allowed him to stay in the park.

"What the hell was wrong with that bear?" Dexter asked the boy what he was talking about. "They don't normally act like that, do they? I mean, I've seen them on television a million times, and they don't run at people. Why the hell did that thing come after me?"

"Because, believe it or not, he is native to this area, and you're in his domain. And they act like wild animals — which is what they are — when they find idiots trying to take selfies with them when all they want to do is to be left alone. Do you realize that you could have been killed by either of those animals?"

The kid mumbled about the fact that he'd seen them on television, and they never acted like that. Then he asked if he was going to be put down. "No, it's against the law for me to put down idiots that come to this park and think they can do whatever they want while here."

"No, I meant the bear. Why aren't they locked up when there are people around? That thing even took my backpack. What the hell is it going to do with that? Wear it or something?" Dexter told him that he'd more than likely tear it apart looking for food or something. "I paid over a thousand bucks for that thing. You'd better be thinking of a way to get me one back if he does that. Now that you mention it, why the hell wasn't he in a cage or something? Don't you lock these monsters up at some point in the day?"

"No. Like I said to you before. This is their land, and we're only visitors to it." Helping the boy up from the ground, Dexter noticed that not only had some other rangers joined him, but his grandda was standing there as well. "You're just lucky that neither one of them decided to kill the lot of you."

The kids would be escorted out of the park and then band for the rest of their stay here. More than likely, they'd be told they could never return, but that was a hard thing to make work. There were a great many people coming in daily, and watching out for them would be difficult.

Going on his next tour, only about ten minutes later than he'd planned it to be, Dexter was glad his new group had heard about the incident and were leery of their surroundings. That was good. Everyone needed to be aware of the things that were going on around them to be safe. As soon as they made it to Laurel falls, Dexter felt like he'd run a marathon. Twice.

There were so many people at the falls that it was hard to keep an eye on the people he was with. He did have to tell a few people to get off the rocks as it wasn't a place to hike that was safe, but all in all, it was a good trip. Answering questions, his favorite part of the tours were good too. A few did ask about the incident at the other side of the park—to which he was surprised to find out that word had traveled so quickly — but he said several times that it was the fault of the kids rather than the animals that lived here.

As he was headed back to the office, he heard from David as well as Mark. Mark told him that the teenagers had been taken out of the park and were not to enter again. He told his brother that he thought that was what would happen. David told him he'd like to meet with him and Sunny while they were in DC tomorrow.

"I can do that. However, you'll have to clear it with Sunny. This is her trip, and I'm only going along to be the heavy." David laughed and told him that Sunny had said the same thing to him. "Good to know that we're on the same page with this. However, I will tell you this, she'd my world, and I will do anything, including killing you if it comes to her getting hurt."

"Again, she said the same thing. I'll make some arrangements to have dinner with the two of you and get back to you. I think the two of you are going to be a wonderful couple." Thanking him, he was glad they were going to meet up with this man. Just to get things cleared up so they could get on with their lives. "Also, I wanted to tell you that Diana has been put in a prison hospital. She won't be getting out unless it's by death."

"Thanks for letting me know about that too." He didn't tell the man that he had already figured that out but let it go. "I'm going to be getting off work soon, so if you need anything else from me, I'll be at home with Sunny. And if you don't mind, unless it's extremely important, don't bother calling us there. I'm going to be too busy wooing my mate to answer or be told anything that can wait until another time."

The man was still laughing when Dexter hung up. As he was entering the office again, he was greeted by not just Mark and Ewing but Barron. They were getting their assignments the same as he was for the rest of the day.

Hugging them all, he was glad now more than ever that he had such a close family and that they all got along so well. He couldn't wait until they were all as happy as he was right now and was thrilled when he was able to sit and talk to them while waiting for the end of his shift. There were no more tours assigned for the day, and he was happy about that.

~*~

Sunny was ready for Dexter when he got home. She had thought about getting her something sexy to wear, but she didn't want to have to waste money on such an extravagance. Nor did she think he'd notice it if she were to have it on. Being just as needy as he was, she was hoping to have him naked about the time he put his foot on the first step of the stairs to their bedroom.

Tomorrow they were going to be picked up around ten in the morning and be in Washington about an hour later. Once there, she had a crew that was going to meet them at the house that would pack up everything. Some of it would come home with them, and the rest would be donated to whatever cause was closest to them when they were finished up.

First, dinner with David and his boss. After

that, they were going to be treated to a play that was in town. Then tomorrow, she and Dexter were going to figure out some things that needed to be done to make them a couple. Filing their marriage paperwork was going to be done. She didn't want a big wedding, if any at all, but she knew they'd have to have proof of marriage if she wanted to have him on her deeds and accounts.

Hearing the crunch of gravel, Sunny was disappointed to see that a truck was coming up the lane to the house and it was making a delivery. While she didn't really care what was being brought up here, she was dismayed to find out that some of the items were hers. She wasn't ready for her stuff yet.

After figuring out that it was computer equipment that had to be set up, she had the person put all the boxes in the basement. Not that she was worried about anyone stealing the things, but she didn't want to have to mess with them today. Or the next few days, for that matter. As soon as the equipment was put away, she waited for Dexter again.

There were plenty of things that she could be doing right now, she supposed. Dexter didn't get off for another hour, but she wanted him now. Laughing at herself, she made her way over to his Grandparents' home as they were both home.

"How about a cup of tea?" She didn't really care for tea but didn't want to turn anything down from the wonderful couple. "You can say no, Sunny. It's all right. Do you want a cup or not? No big deal if you don't."

"I don't care for hot tea." Nodding, Grannie poured herself and grandda one. "Wow, what is that? It smells like fresh spring flowers."

"It is, as a matter of fact. We go hunting in the early spring for certain flowers to dry and use. Then, in the later part of summer into fall, we find other flowers to which we do the same thing. My goodness, you should taste my pumpkin acorn tea. It's the best that I've ever made. To me anyway." She spent the next hour tasting teas that had been made by Grannie and Grandda. When Dexter arrived home, he came over too, and they had cookies and tea until dinnertime. They decided to cook out, and the others that could make it showed up too.

As they were making their way back to the house, he stopped in the middle of the yard and bent on one knee before her. She didn't say a word to him, not even sure that what she was thinking was going to happen was it.

"Will you marry me? I could go into all this mushy stuff, but I don't think you'd go for that." She told him to do it. "All right. I love you with every breath I take. I can't imagine a life without you in it. Even before you came into my life, I knew that once you were here, that my life would be perfect. And it is so much more than that. You're all I have ever wanted in a mate. More than anyone in the world could have hoped for when they found someone to love."

"That wasn't too bad." He kissed her hand and pulled out a ring from his shirt pocket. "Oh, Dexter, that's beautiful." Dexter smiled and asked her if that was a yes. "Yes. I'll marry you. So long as you know that in my heart, I'm already a part of you."

The ring fit her perfectly. It was beautiful like she had said, but when she looked at it closer, she thought there weren't enough words to tell him how beautiful it was. The diamond was large, and it was surrounded by smaller diamonds on a tiffany setting. When he stood up, Sunny pulled him to her and kissed him with all the love that she had for him.

"You keep that up, and we're not going to make it to the house." Picking her up, he carried her to the house. He didn't bother putting her down but carried her all the way to their bedroom. After setting her on her feet again, he kissed her this time. "I love you, Sunshine Cross. With all that I am."

"And I love you. I will love you until the day I die and beyond." This time when they kissed, it was different. It wasn't so much hungry but exploring too. Dexter began taking her clothing off as he kissed her bare skin. "You're taking too long, buster. I've been wanting to get you naked all day. Shit, or get off the pot."

His laughter made her smile. "You have such a romantic...no, not romantic but sort of. I think you're going to keep me on my toes for a very long time, love." She said that she hoped so. "As do I."

When he had her shirt off, she started to undo the buttons on his shirt. Sunny was glad that he'd changed into his regular clothing. It made it so much easier to get him naked. And she wanted him naked in the worse sort of way.

The touching was wonderful. Each place that she touched him, his skin was warm. It tasted so strong and sweet to her. He tasted of the earth but in a good way. Like a refreshing rain storm, and the earth was still damp.

"I need you." She told Dexter that she needed him as well. When he lifted her up, tearing the last of her clothing off of her, she took his mouth hard. Screaming when he shoved her against the wall, his cock filled her so tightly that she was sure that she was going to be sore tomorrow. Then he took her to their bed and laid her down. His body was still a part of her own.

As Dexter held her to him, his body moved slowly in and out of hers. She felt like she was being made love to. Not sex, not anything like just sex but making love. His hands were everywhere. His mouth followed. Even when he nipped at her flesh, his tongue would make the tiny wound feel better.

Sunny massaged his shoulders as she held onto them. Kissed his muscles too. When he lifted her up from the bed by her bottom, she felt a tightness in her body that seemed to come from her very core. He filled her so nicely that she came three times before she could catch her breath.

"You like that?" Nodding, Sunny wrapped her legs around his hips. "Yes, that's it, love. Hold me to you."

She came so many times that she lost count. Almost as soon as one climax was finished, he'd bring her over a peak that would have her coming again. Sunny saw stars and rainbows. A couple of times, she could have sworn that she came apart only to be slammed back together. And through it all, she told Dexter how much she loved him. How she wanted to have his children. She wanted to make a full life with him.

As soon as he wrapped both her hands into his, she held onto the headboard as he moved over her body. Each time he could nip at her skin, like before, he would soothe it by kissing where he'd bitten her.

"I need to fill you." Her body shivered at his words. Her pussy was soaked with need when he moved atop her again. "come for me, Sunshine. Please, I want to feel you tighten around my cock while I fill you."

Nothing could have prepared her for coming with him. She knew that, on some level, she was going to be hoarse tomorrow but didn't care as she screamed out her releases. It wasn't just one, either. Her body came again and again while feeling turned inside out. Even as he came deep inside of her, it was like she was being given a great gift. Magically feelings entered into her body and made her limp too.

When Dexter dropped atop her, she couldn't have moved if the house had caught fire. Small twinges of climaxes took her breath away. Her heart was pounding so hard that she was positive that she was going to be dead in her next breath. Closing her eyes, she simply slipped away. Her body was so relaxed.

Waking up when the bed shifted, Dexter told her that he'd be right back. Nodding, she thought she had anyway, sleep took her under once again. Waking again, the room was bright with light, and she was alone in bed. Reaching out for Dexter, he asked her if she could call him instead. Sunny could feel the tension in his voice. She called him, and while she didn't know what was going on, she could tell that there was something. Sunny asked him if he needed her with him.

"Jamie and her dogs are here helping. We have a missing woman." She said that she was coming to him. "I'm at the office coordinating the rangers while the others are setting up roadblocks."

"Was she kidnapped?" He said that they didn't know. That she had been at a local hotel with her family until yesterday morning. Now there is no sign of her. "Her family didn't know to call sooner? That's messed up."

"They're all dead." She told him she was sorry. "No need for that, love. But I think we can use your help. I've been playing around with being a hawk to see over things that others can't, and I'm going to go out as soon as my grandda gets here. If you could join me, that would be wonderful."

"Have something there that I can touch." He asked her if she thought she could find the woman that way. "I don't know. I could just a little before, but I think I'm stronger. I know that Jamie and her dogs do the same thing, finding a scent but perhaps I can help with that as well."

"We'll take anything that we can at this point." She said she'd be there in twenty minutes and was glad when she made it just in time to help out with the search. The news that she was hearing on the way in didn't bode well for the mother of three who had come here with her new husband and her own children. Almost as soon as Sunny touched the hairbrush, she wanted to sob out the injustice of it all.

She looked at Jamie when she said her name. "Don't say anything just yet." Nodding, she did ask her why not. *"The press is here, and we don't want to say anything just yet. They're looking for the killer. Unless you know who it might be."*

"Her ex-husband. He killed them all. The woman and her new family got away from him for abuse. He found them and then killed them all. The mentality of, if I can't have them, then no one will. He's dead too." Jamie nodded, and they took the dogs to find the woman's remains. They were far enough away now that they could speak freely. "You know, sometimes I really hate that I can do this."

"I understand that perfectly. But I'm glad that you and I can work together on this." As they made their way to the site where the woman's body was, they talked about working together on all sorts of projects like this one. "That way, we can validate with the dogs where the bodies are found."

"I'd like that." When they found the body, she was in terrible shape. It looked as if he had tortured her until she finally died. His body was hanging from the rafters of the barn not far from where the body of the woman had been found. "Such a waste of human flesh."

Chapter 3

David was happy to see the couple. He was even happier to know that the two of them were in love. It was as obvious as the noses on their faces that they were in love, and he couldn't be happier for them both.

"You've called us here, dumbass. Stop looking at us like we're the next best thing to sliced ham on rye. Which I'm hungry for now. As I have said to you a million times, shit or get off the pot. We have shit to do today, and you're not helping." He grinned at Sunny. "That's not getting you any points for me not killing you where you stand. Get to explaining why we're here."

"The president is on his way to talk to you two as well." She said she didn't have time for this. "No. But he does, and I would like to suggest, not order you but suggest that you wait around for what he has to say to the two of you."

"What's this all about? I thought we were here so you could tell me what's going on with her job." David told Dexter that it was more than that. "More what? We really have a great deal to do today. We're going to go to her home and figure out what she wants to keep or not."

The president walked through the door and acknowledged David. "We're going to buy it and keep it ready for when you need to come here. Hello, Sunshine. And it's good to meet you, Dexter." The man sat down next to Dexter and smiled at the couple. David wanted to tell him to back off, but he thought it might go over better for all of them when Roger figured out for himself that Sunny was not one to fuck with. When she stood up, he did as well. "Are you going to leave now that I've arrived? That's not very nice, do you think?"

"I've been pissing around here for the last hour waiting on more information than I have now. And you come in here, like you're in charge and tell me that you're going to be buying my home, which I never said was for sale and making it so that what? I have a place to visit when you get up off your collective asses and decide that you need me again? No. It doesn't work that way for me. My contract ends for you guys in four months. Seems like a waste of tax papers money to buy a house only to have no one coming to live in it."

"Are you always this toxic?" Sunny said he'd caught her on a good day as she wasn't nearly as toxic as she usually was. "Sit down."

"Fuck you." As she was getting up to leave, Dexter only stood up. David thought for sure that the younger man was going to shift, but all he did was lean toward Roger and smile.

"You pull shit like this again, and I will have a bruin on your ass so quickly that you'll never see us coming. And that lovely wife of yours will never find enough for you to be put into a baggie. Do I make myself clear?" He told him that he was the president. "I don't give a good damn if you're the almighty lord. You fuck with my mate again, and I will take you out of this world."

They were both gone for a few minutes when Roger turned to David. "I screwed this up, I'm thinking." David didn't bother answering him. "I see. Keeping it close to the vest, are you? Well, I need to fix this. Any ideas how I should do that?"

"I'd say that I'd just back off. But I know you better than that. Just let her come to you. One thing that I've learned over the years of working with Sunny is that she will come back here to apologize to you for talking to you that way. She always does." Roger asked him about Dexter. "I'd believe every word he said to you. However, I'd not expect him to come back here with even a hint of an apology on his lips. He's pissed off, and I don't really blame him. He won't tell her what to do until she asks, but Sunny is in love with that man, and if you hurt him, I think she'll do worse by you than he said he'd do to you."

Roger leaned back in the chair that he'd taken

when he'd arrived. He was at a loss on how to proceed. "I wanted to show her that I wasn't going to be taking any shit from her. I have a feeling all I did was make her more pissed off than she usually is." David told him he thought that was about right. "I don't know what to do. Any suggestions?"

"Have Emmy talk to her. Your wife could and has charmed the worse kind of men that came to you pissed off. I know that Emmy and Sunny are friends. Have been since before you married her." He said that Emmy was going to be pissed off that he'd done this to her. "That is a given. You've managed to piss off two women that you need in your life. And I think you'd better get it fixed before either one of them decided to do what they said they would to you. I know that I'd say to be more afraid of Sunny than your wife, but I'd say that if you're smart, which I think you might be, then you'll make this up to Dexter too. He's a powerful man, and his brother is the bruin king. Fuck this up, Roger, and you won't live to regret it."

"Christ. I should have just done what Emmy

told me to do. She is going to be pissed off." The woman in question came into the room and sat down in the chair across from her husband. David started to leave, but all she did was look at him, and he sat back down. "I messed up."

She cocked an eyebrow at her husband. "Do you think? What do you think I thought when I called her to ask her if we could get together for lunch tomorrow, and she told me so long as you didn't go. Then, Christ, Roger, you fucked up when you tried to be all macho. I told you it wouldn't work. She's not like other women. You can't pull that shit on her." He said he didn't think she was like other men, either. "Yet you treated her like she was nothing but shit under your shoes." He said that's now what he intended. "Be that as it may, I'm going to go over to her home and have lunch with her and her lovely husband. You, my dear husband, are not invited. And you are not to interfere or so help me, I'll have you for lunch. What a thing to start off with her. Did you really think that—well, of course, you did. You always think that being a hard-ass is the only way to go. See what it got you? Nothing, that's what."

After she left, David couldn't help it. He burst out laughing. And couldn't stop himself from laughing more every time he looked at Roger. Roger asked him what the hell he thought was so funny.

"You. Not only have you been told off by the one person that you can or could have depended on to have your back, but you also pissed off her mate and his bruin, if I'm not mistaken as well as your wife." He looked at his watch, then laughed harder. "All that in twenty minutes, and it's not even noon yet. What do you have planned for the rest of your day, Roger? Are you going to bring Armageddon down on the earth? It wouldn't surprise me in the least bit if that was your plan."

After he growled, David got up and left him there. It wasn't often that Roger messed up, but when he did, it was a doozy. Today, a rarity in his messing up so badly tickled David. He hadn't any idea why he found it so funny that he had this time, but he was going to enjoy it as much as he could. Tomorrow things would be worked out, but for now, it was funny.

David did call Dexter to talk to him about some of the things that he needed to get cleared up. They were going to convince the man to come and work for them, but for now, he needed to clear up some things that he'd found out about his family. Nothing major, but just to talk to the other man.

"I don't know my parents at all. My grandparents raised us when we were just kids after they died. Why is it important that you know about my father's education?" He told him what he'd been thinking about. Also mentioned the job. "I see."

He had a feeling that Dexter was ready to hang up his ranger hat and try something else for a change. David didn't push it but only asked if he could talk to his grandparents and see what they had to say about his father graduating at the top of his class from Harvard, yet there wasn't any kind of recognition mentioned in the paper. Just a query, nothing more.

"Grandda said that he didn't want anyone to know that he'd done so well. I also talked to my older brother, who said he thought dad would have done that. He seemed to hate to be singled out. If it makes any difference to you, I did the same thing as my brothers in graduating with honors in college. Our grandparents pushed us to be the best we could be, and we did that as best we could for them. What do you mean, you might well have a job for me?" He told him a little of what it would entail, working for the government. "I do that already. Keep the citizens safe at the park. I'm qualified with a handgun as well as a rifle."

"This would be more like a Secret Service sort of job. But not with the president or his first lady. But more in the capacity of being alert to their surroundings. All the people that work for us are well trained as well as smart, but they lack the skills of being attuned to things going on around them. Blending in, I guess you could call it. I'm to understand that in addition to being a Park Ranger for so long that you did a stint in the service as an undercover agent. How did that work for you? And why did you leave?"

"I was asked to leave when it was apparent

that I wasn't human." He could hear the anger in Dexter's voice but didn't push him. "When I was out on a mission, and I survived, they thought that there would be too many questions for me not to be able to answer them. So they, not so politely, asked me to resign. I did."

"We could care less what you are so long as the job gets done." Dexter snorted. "Yes, well, I guess I can understand your not believing me on that. But I'd like the opportunity to talk to you and Sunny about it."

"Will jackass be there?" He said that he'd make sure that he wasn't. "I don't care that he is or not, but he will be polite. I wasn't shitting him when I told him not to piss off Sunny again. It took me half an hour to get her calm enough to talk to me about her home. It's a nice one too."

"It is. I've been there a few times when her parents were alive and since then too. It's been in Sunny's family for a while now, and I think that she could, if she really wanted to make a killing off of selling it. I'm not saying that she shouldn't, but as you've no doubt noticed, it's a huge house, and it would be good for your family to visit here and not have to worry about having hotel rooms or anything like that. There are cars there, too, if I remember correctly." Dexter said that there was and a limo service as well. "Yes, the Meadows were quite wealthy when they were living around here. Your family is as well, but she had a good bit more. And she's very old money. Not that it matters for me, but I've heard that said about them. From what I heard, they held the best parties around. And were as generous as they were wealthy. Charities clamored to have them host a fundraiser for them."

"Emmy Jackson just showed up. Does she come and go as she wants? That seems sort of dangerous if you ask me." He asked the younger man if he thought she wasn't safe with him and Sunny. "Now that you mention it, I'd say she's safer. All right. I'll talk to Sunny about the job. But for now, I'd like it if you were to keep the president at bay. We were excited to come here and make some progress. I don't want to have to kill him for making my mate upset like she was before. And I will."

"I'll have a talk to him. Emmy is there to smooth things over." He said that he'd figured that out already. "Yes, I'm sure that Emmy was very vocal about how she was pissed off at her husband as well. They're a good couple, the two of them. But when he goes against her advice, things don't bode well for him. Not that she wears the pants in the family, but the saying is true when they say opposites attract. Those two couldn't be more different. They balance things out. Which is usually good for the country."

"He really pissed us off. Where does he get off acting like he's in charge of our personal life? Yes, I get that he's the president, but she is really talking about quitting what she does for them. And I don't have a clue what she does, but I'd have to agree with her about it." He said that he'd planned on explaining it to him when they'd gotten here. "If it's all right with Sunny, you can come over for dinner tonight, and we'll get into that. We have plans for tomorrow to get things settled with the house. Don't bring that up. I mean, unless you want to be set out on your ass,

I'd leave it until she brings it up."

"I can do that." They talked about dinner and what time he should show up. He was looking forward to it as much as he had been anything in a long time. To be able to share what he knew about the young woman with her mate was going to be epic. Dexter was in for a big surprise when it came to how helpful and useful Sunny was to the United States government.

~*~

"You're making it sound like I'm special. When I'm not." Dexter laughed when Sunny said that to David. "I just go into a situation, tag the person that is to be taken out, and that's all."

"I have a feeling that it's much more than that." David told him that it was so much more than that. "When you say that you tag the target, what is it that you do? I mean, do you just point them out?"

"No. Well, sort of. I have this ability to just touch them in a way that marks them. Let me think a moment on how to tell you what it is that I do." She got up to pace, and Dexter thought her the most beautiful creature in the world. Even when she was pissed off, she was simply the most beautiful woman in the world to him. "I used to take in this little device that would mark the person as the target. But that got to be a pain in the ass. Sometimes they'd put on a jacket or a coat, and that would block the target mechanism." She paced more, and he thought of something.

"You came up with a better way to mark them. I'm guessing that being an elite shifter, it would have been easy to come up with a better plan." She smiled at him. "I love when you look at me like that. I feel so smart."

"You're very smart, ass hole." She laughed when he did. "Yes, I figured out that I could use a little of my magic and make them have a mark on them. Not just their clothing as I was doing before but a mark that would show up even if they were to cover it up. They would be targeted better that way so that no one else would be. Like if the mechanism were to fall off and be picked up by someone else. This was a permanent mark that only the person on the other end could see with a special sort of magic that I would share with them."

"And with this magic, you pinpoint the targets that — I'm assuming these people are bad guys that were presumably killed later." She said that she'd not asked but assumed that was so. Dexter looked at David, and he nodded. He explained what else her marking the people would mean. "I can see that. You'd be able to follow his or her every move with a mark like that. Is there more? Not that what she does now isn't enough, but I have a feeling that it's more than that."

"As when you put me in your pocket to get me out of the hospital safely, I can enter homes when no one else can. Not to mark this time but to have a look around to see if they're actually holding someone that we're looking for. Also, how the household is treated when there have been concerns of abuse. Most of those complaints are domestic, but there needs to be accountability when it's voiced so strongly." He asked her if she enjoyed that. "Yes. Not what I find when I get into some houses but that I can be helpful.

This magic that I have, it makes it so that I can get in and out of a house if there is a suspect of a bomb or some other kind of device that might well get others hurt." She turned and looked at him. "You'll be able to help me with this if I still want to work for them. Right?"

"I'll do whatever needs to be done to keep you safe. And if that means that I go with you as a mouse, then I'll do it. However, I have little to no training on how to be a mouse." Sunny sat down on his lap, and he held her as he asked his next question of David. "I'm assuming that the president hasn't any idea what the extent of her ability is. Does he?"

"He does, as a matter of fact. That's why I was as surprised as you were about how he came into the meeting today." David leaned back in his chair as he looked at the two of them. "Roger is a good man. But I think he gets a little overwhelmed when it comes to making sure that things are in a neat row. His anger, at times, spills out of his mouth before he has a chance to figure out that sometimes nicer is better than being a bully. I've spoken to him just so you're aware of it. So has Emmy. I would expect a call from him soon. And a great deal of groveling too."

"He was insufferable. More than that, he was a jackass too. No one talks to me like he does and gets away with it. I work hard for him and everyone else. There wasn't any reason for him to be a fucking bastard when I was there on my own time. That's as good a reason for me to quit the job that I've been doing better than anything else. I still might do it." David slid a file across to the two of them. "What the fuck is this? I just told you that I didn't know if I was going to continue to work for the government anymore."

"It's your new perks for working for us. In fact, one of them is a raise you should have been given to you some time ago. Your new pay rate, as well as a check covering the retro amount you should have been given, is in there as well. Additionally, you'll have better coverage of insurance and other things such as life and medical on your and Dexter's family too. They'll be included in all that you get as well." Dexter didn't say anything when he opened the file and saw just how much of a retro amount for back pay she was getting. He was skimming the other paperwork when David continued. "There will be a car as well as a jet at your disposal. That includes your family as well, Dexter. It's not just to be used for business only, either. It's there for the family to make use of. When you're all happy, I know that all of the world will be sighing a great sigh of relief too. Even if they don't know who is out there for them. Medical for the family as well as cart Blanc on all things that you might need for your jobs since you all essentially work for us anyway. And by us, I'm saying the American people. You're a good family, come from good stock. I'd be honored to have you out there working for us. Not that John Q. Public knows about your job with me, but I will, and that makes me prouder than a speckled pup under a little red wagon. My daddy used to say that all the time."

"It says here that we'll be asked to come to all events given at the White House. I'm assuming that you mean Sunny on this." David laughed and said that it, too, was for his entire family. "I'm sure you should rethink that. My family is a bunch of bears that wouldn't know which fork to use in a formal setting."

"You'll all do fine, I'm sure of it." Sunny kissed him on the mouth and told him she'd be proud to have them all there with the other big shits. He thanked her for that. "All right. You have the paperwork there that you will need to be made aware of for now. But if you have any questions, you only need to give me a call, day or night, and I'll be able to answer them. If there is anything that I can't answer, then I'll find you someone that can."

After he left, neither of them moved. The house was wonderful, and he loved it. Not that he would trade living on the mountain, but this was a huge house, and he didn't feel as closed in as when he had been in other houses when visiting friends. Sunny asked him what he wanted to do now.

"I'm not sure what you mean by that. Do you mean about the job? I think that the ball is in your court. I'm not going to work for them if you're not there as well. I have been thinking about leaving the

Ranger job for a bit now. I do well at blowing glass when I have time, and I was thinking about just doing that for a time. Not forever, but at least for a little while. What do you think about all this?" She said she didn't know. "I can understand that as well. It's a lot to take in. He didn't say that it was important to give him an answer right away, so we should just take a few days and think about it. What do you say to that?"

"Yes. I like that idea much better. It is a lot to take in. Especially with your family being involved. I'd like to say that they would enjoy it, but I'm not sure that your grandparents will enjoy coming off the mountain to be around a bunch of shits that she can't wring their necks. I saw her doing that to a chicken the other day, and I'd never want to be on the receiving end of that sort of killing. Then she cooked it up for dinner like it wasn't a big deal. It was good, don't get me wrong. But nope, not going to piss her off."

"The rooster." She nodded. "Yeah, she told me that he pecked her a couple of times, and she had had enough of his shit. Not like that, of course. Grannie is very soft-spoken, but he was trouble since the day he figured out that he had a harem of chicks of his own. The rooster that she has now is small yet, but he's doing a good job."

"She more than likely let him see what she'd done to the other rooster, and of course, he'll be on his best behavior." She stood up and stretched, and so did his cock. "I have some things here that I'd like to take back to your grannie. The last time I was here, I found some of my grandmother's blankets that she had made. They're stained in a few places and worn in a few more. Grannie told me that she has a way to get them cleaned up, and she'll do the repairs on them as well. I think she'll do a fine job."

"Grandda said that you have a bunch of artifacts that were around here when your home was built. He seemed to think that you were going to be bringing them home with you so that he could date them for you. He loves that sort of thing. So does Jamie's dad. They're forever with their metal detectors out and about looking for things to dig up." Sunny told him how they'd taken her to the shop that all of them contributed to. It was full of all kinds of stuff. "Yes, we all have something that we do. Mine, as you know, is glass blowing. Gibb is the only real gardener next to Grannie. Even though we have plenty of money for food and such, the two of them plant this massive garden every summer that we eat on throughout the winter months. Frazier is a hell of a woodworker. He mostly does art things of the mountain. Ewing makes wine and uses my bottles to bottle it up. But it's Barron that has the most success at what he does for a side job. He makes goat cheese that he sells all over the country, as well as smoked sausages that sells too. I love his herb cheese the most."

"I've had it. At an event here in DC, I think. It was on a platter with other things that I couldn't get enough of. And crackers. If you tell me that someone in our family made them, I'm going to be sleeping with them too in order to get all that I want." He laughed. "Laugh it up. But those were the best I've ever eaten since then too. They had oats and barley in them. Please tell me that someone in your family is that talented.

"Grannie. She hated the crackers that they offered at home. Mostly they would have to go with name brands to satisfy the tourist. But they sell well in the shop. Mountain Grown has been around since before I was born. And I'm sure that it will continue on even after we're all pushing up daisies." She said she was going to make sure that they had them here when we were staying. "So we're going to be working with the government?"

"I can't turn it down. I'm good at it, and I save a lot of lives with what I can do. And with your help and knowing that your family is safe from others makes it easier for me to go on these types of missions and not worry if anyone will miss me if I get hurt." He said he'd protect her and would die without her. "I know that too, but just knowing that you're going to be there with me makes it so much better for my peace of mind. I've enjoyed just hanging around with your family and the households. And I love your grandparents too."

"They love you as well. My whole family does.

Jamie and even her dogs are in love with you." She asked him if he loved her. "With every breath I take, I love you all the more."

They decided not to take too much to the house in the Smokies. They would need to have a residence here fully stocked, and the staff would be paid all the time through the government. He did wonder at the extravagance of what they were doing for them but figured they knew that they had in her more than he did. He had to work out giving his notice at the Ranger office and figure out what he was going to be doing after that. He might just become a lazy bum for a few weeks to get to know his new mate. That had its perks too.

Going up to the upper levels, she showed him where to find the things they'd take back to his family. He was surprised to see the extensive collection of things that had been found on the land where the house was, and he knew that his grannie would do a good job on the blankets that had been handmade. Even taking her home some of the pictures of the house as it was being built would tickle his grandda a great deal.

"Mr. Cross, there is a call for you on line three." He nodded at the butler, then asked him if he knew who it was. "He said that he was a friend of yours from college but nothing more. It would be a great pleasure for me to just tell him that you're unavailable. I don't know who put it in the local paper about the two of you getting married, but that will bring out people saying all kinds of things about how they're friends with you and the misses."

"From now on, if they have nothing more to say to you than that they know me or Sunny, then you have my permission to tell them to fuck off." Todd, the butler, laughed a little before catching himself. "My family are all bears. I don't know if you were aware of that, but if there is an emergency from one of them, they have a faster and better way of contacting me. If anyone gives you any trouble, you just let me know. I want this house and the one we have near my family to be a safe place for us to go without being bothered."

"Thank you, sir. Also, as per the wishes of

Ms. Sunny, we're having all the rooms in the house updated and cleaned. In the event that your family comes to visit. Also, do you know if there are things that they will not eat?" He told him what he knew about their eating habits which was that they'd eat just about anything. "I thought as much. Thank you, sir."

After Todd left them, Dexter realized that he'd been armed. He asked Sunny if the rest of the staff was, and she said that they were. Washington wasn't a safe place to be with all the shit going on all the time. "I'll make sure that I'm armed all the time as well. I'm assuming that you have a gun safe here on the land?"

"Two of them. One is on the main floor, hidden by a wall, and the other is out in the barn that holds the tractor and things for the house. They're both large in capacity, but they're not loaded up as yet. We'll have to take care of that as well. Also, I don't know if I made you aware of this or not, but the house had twenty bedrooms in it. There are also twenty-four bathrooms. Each of the bedrooms along the wings are suites that connect if it's necessary." He only shook his head. "As you were told before, my family has been a part of this area for a great long time and would hold parties that had people staying over rather than driving home. Also, my grandmother would house families when they were, for one reason or another, homeless. This house has seen a great deal over the centuries."

They spoke about the things that they needed to get done while here. About nine o'clock, Roger called and talked to him first, then Sunny. Leaving them to their conversation, Dexter made his way outside to look around. The yard was well maintained. Just as he was looking around the wings, he noticed the armed men roaming around. He'd have to find out who they were with before they went to bed. He didn't want any surprises when they were making love later.

Chapter 4

Grace wasn't entirely sure why they were making such a fuss about her defending herself. She'd not so much as defended herself but was trying to make her point clear to the dumbass. Not only did she have to endure being put in jail for something that she felt justified in doing, but they were telling her that she wasn't going to be able to go home until the trial was over. Then she might well be here longer as she might be going to jail for a good deal longer. Stupid cow. Had she only just—

"Ms. Hardgrave, are you listening to what is going on?" She said that she didn't care, telling the judge that she had been arrested falsely. "Not according to the report that I have before me. You were arrested for assaulting a woman by the name of Sunshine Meadow Cross."

"She was bulling me into moving. I have every right to stand where I want, as it's my right as a citizen of the United States. Not to mention, she was rude to me. And listening in on my conversation with the people that I was speaking to." The judge asked her if she knew she was blocking several hundred people from going up or down the trail. "So? I was there and doing what I needed at the time. Where did she get off thinking that she was more important than me having a private conversation? She isn't just so we're clear on that. I needed to make those people that I was speaking to aware that they weren't the only ones on the trail. That everyone should just go home and let me do what I want when I need to. You'd think that this park wasn't something that you can see on the internet the way that they were crowding me on the pathway up and down. Why don't they just have one or two people go up at a time then there wouldn't be any trouble with people crowding me? That would save a great deal of heartache if you asked me."

"No one did ask you." He looked around the room and called on a Ranger by the name of Cross. "Mark, could you please give me an estimate on how many people visit the park in which you work a year?"

"Over fourteen million in the last year, sir. That would average about forty thousand per day, but that's over a year's time. The visitors are fewer in the winter months, though we are still open for the entire year." He asked him how many would he estimate would be on the day that the officer was harmed. "We have that estimate at eighty thousand visitors, sir."

"The park had to close down that particular area, am I right?" The Ranger, or whatever he was, said that it was still closed off due to the trial. "I see. And how many men are watching that area for the park? I'm assuming that there are quite a few of them."

"Yes, sir." The man was confusing her, but she let him prattle on about visitors to the park. She still liked her idea of having one group go up and down at a time. How much time that would save for her when she had to get out more. Stupid doctor. This was his fault. "Yes, sir, I'd say that we have about ten rangers and volunteers on duty at all times."

"Sounds like a great deal of overtime. I won't even ask you how much—" Grace stood up, glad now that she hadn't been chained like the other people in the courtroom were. She had a good mind to just leave. What could they do to her anyway? Nothing, that's what.

"What the hell are you going on about? This is getting ridiculous. I want to get out of here so that I can get on with my life. I have things to take care of." The judge told her to hush up. "Hush up? What am I ten? You'll not speak to me that way. I have rights too. What does it matter to you how much overtime has been generated on this incident that I'm supposed to have caused? Nothing."

"Oh, but it does. You're the cause of the overtime, and I plan on making sure that you reimburse the park for—" She cut him off only to be told to shut up again. "I'm in charge here, and I'll talk when I feel the need to explain things to you. You should know what it feels like being on the other end of having people explain things to you. Now, as I was saying, you're going to be put in a position of paying back the park for the overtime that you endured for them when you decided to turn a pathway into a crime scene."

"She didn't die. I mean, more the pity on that, but she didn't die. I only showed her what she needed to learn about being rude. If more people did that to their children, this would be a better place for all of us. Now, what do I have to do to get out of here? I'm sick of asking this question only to be fobbed off." He told her that perhaps she should be asking where she was going when this was over. "Home is where I'm going, you moron. I've done nothing wrong here, and I'm sorely tired of telling you idiots that. She only had to wait until I was finished taking those other people to task before she so rudely interrupted me."

"It's not your job, believe it or not, to take

anyone to task. Now, as I was talking to the ranger here, it looks like you're going to be paying the park for a great deal of money." She said she wasn't paying anything as the park should have taken care that she didn't have to do their job for them. "Making sure that people aren't doing as they please when they're being rude on the trails. This is not your job. Why do I even have to explain this to you?"

"You should know that this park is overcrowded and undermanaged. Someone needs to take charge. I was only doing my civic duty. They should be paying me for what I did that day. I not only got the trail cleared of hoodlums, but I also made a few people — that woman being one of them — understand that being rude to someone isn't going to get her anywhere but in trouble. I'm not going to be putting up with anyone treating me like she did that day."

"It's funny you should mention that. It seems that the town that you're from isn't the least bit surprised to find out that you've been arrested for being rude to people. The paperboy was only the last of your victims when you got a burr up your butt about him not ironing your newspaper before he brought it to you. Not only did you hit him with that cane you are so proud of, but you've also been known to use it on people in church when they have a child with them that is upset. And it's also been brought to my attention that the grocery store where you used to shop has a picture of your face on their front doors as well as at every register that says that they're not to engage with you if you're in the store but to call the police. Shall I go on?" She told him he was a waste of air. "Perhaps. But there is a long list of things here that have been brought up against you now that you're in jail. I'm not going to bother with reading them all, but this one, in particular, is very telling. Did you really threaten a child with prison time in his own yard about being too loud when he was laughing?"

"Yes. I did try and tell his stupid parents that I liked it quiet during the daylight hours, but they insisted on putting that brat in the back yard with that dog. Christ, it wasn't bad enough that the dumbass dog was barking all the time when it was out, but that kid's laughter just grated on my nerves. Why wasn't it locked into the house instead of being out where I could hear it? I'll tell you why, because they were as stupid as the kid was." She laughed when she thought of their faces when she put a for sale sign in their yard. "I tried to buy the house from them to get them to move, but they wouldn't sell. Whatever happened after that was their own problem. I had warned them several times."

"You slashed their tires. Threw rocks at the child in question. As well as you poisoned their dog." She had been trying to poison the child, but the dog got to it first. But of course, she didn't tell him that. Grace wasn't that stupid. "Then it says here that you threatened them with burning down their home if they pressed charges. What sort of person doesn't care for the laughter of children?"

"Me. And I'm entitled to my likes and dislikes. Everyone certainly does shove theirs onto me. Did you know that they plant flowers in the main street baskets and get pissy when someone comes along and takes one home for their front yard? Doesn't my taxes pay for those stupid things? I should be entitled to take as many as I want. They certainly do charge me enough in taxes."

"Which you don't pay. But we're getting off the subject here. Ms. Hardgrave, I'm charging you with the attempted murder of a Federal Agent by the name of Sunshine Cross. Also, the—" She asked him how that was her fault. "You hit her several times with your cane and also obstructed the medical team from getting to her when she was in need of help."

"She shouldn't have—" The judge told her to shut up again. "I'm not going to put up with you talking to me that way anymore. You'll do as I say, or I'll have to teach you a few lessons as well. The nerve of some people." She looked around for her cane. "Where is my cane? I need that to get around."

"Also, thank you for that, for threatening a federal judge. As for your cane, it's been stored away as evidence. They're finding a lot of unexplained DNA on it. That's sad, really. And it's my understanding that once this is over with, with can't be soon enough for me, it will be destroyed. You'll be remanded over for court in the federal sector, and after that, you'll be taken to prison for a term of imprisonment of not more than thirty years. Along with that, you'll be required to pay the daily costs of the crime scene that you so readily admitted to creating." He asked the man behind her if he'd gotten a total as yet. She must have missed the part where he'd asked him to do that. "All right, you'll be required to pay back the hospital bills that were incurred with Agent Cross as well as the overtime used to keep the scene ready for this trial." When he told her the amount he thought that she should pay, he grinned at her. "Yes, I did say that amount. And you will pay it back while in prison. I've never been so happy to send someone off to prison as I am you. I will tell you that I had it in my head to have you work off your hours in a volunteer capacity, but I thought you'd cause more harm than good. So it's off to prison with you."

She was cuffed like a criminal and taken back to jail before she could demand that he take it all back. When she got into her cell, she was pissed to find that not only hadn't it been cleaned up, and she was no closer to getting her things brought to her from the hotel than she was before she'd gone to the courthouse. The girl, some twit that was wearing a uniform like she was an officer or something, wouldn't give her a straight answer no matter how many times she told her to.

"I asked you a question, girly, and I demand an answer. When am I getting out of here to take care of things? I have a home that I'd like to go to, and my family is going to have to step up and take care of this crap for me." The girl just walked away without a word. "Damn it, I'm putting you on my list of people to have a talking to soon. See that you don't regret this too."

Sitting on the side of the cheap cot that she'd been assigned, she was just thinking of what she was going to do when she got herself an attorney that would sue this entire town. She might even take over the park, for all its lameness and sell it off to the highest bidder. Not that she could see a reason that anyone would want the place. It was filled with morons like the one that had gotten her into this mess. Looking up when someone laughed, she saw the very person she'd been thinking about. She asked her what she wanted.

"Nothing much, I guess, since you've been sentenced. Just to tell you that I'm glad that you're going to be going away. Also, the Pritchels, in the event you ever bothered to know them are your neighbors, are thrilled as well. They've purchased your home so that they can have it torn down and their yard made bigger. Your soon-to-be ex-husband was very generous to them on the price." She told her that her house hadn't been for sale. "You might have missed it when they told you that you'll sell off your worldly goods to pay back what you owe the park while musing about how you've been done wrong by so many people. There is supposed to be a celebration in your town too soon. They're all thrilled that you're going to be going away. I think that we might go, my husband and I. I hadn't realized that you lived so close to the Smokies."

"We'll just see about that, now, won't we? You look fit as a fiddle. Why am I being charged with your attempted murder when you're standing right here? Also, if I had wanted you dead, you'd be that. So tell me why you're really here." A chair was brought to her with only her having to nod in the direction of the doorway, and the woman sat down. "You seem to command a great deal of power. Why don't you use some of that to get me out of here, and I won't have to come after you."

"You're threatening me again. I would have — never mind. I started to say that you would have learned your lesson, but that's not really your style is it? To learn from your mistakes. But I digress. I'm here to tell you that I've spoken to your daughter as well as your son. They've assured me that they want nothing to do with you being in jail. Nor are they likely to come and visit you. Unless they said it would be to make sure that you're actually in prison and not lying to them. Did you do that a great deal? Lie to your kids? Not that it matters. But they've washed their hands of you as has your husband." She said she didn't want anything to do with them either. They didn't listen any better than she did. "I thought you'd say that. I did want to tell you that you have three of the most beautiful granddaughters that I've ever seen. One of them is married and expecting their first child. Also, your son, a good-looking man who must have gotten his looks from his father, is enjoying his life just the way that he's wanted to do. He had three sons that are younger, of course, but happy not having anything to do with you."

"You think I care that my children, ungrateful shits all around, are procreating like rabbits? I don't." The woman just smiled at her. "What else? I know that there is more to it than a bunch of brats that will only crowd up the world more than it is now."

"They could have helped you. Your son and daughter played the lottery some years ago and won it all by themselves. A great deal of money is at their disposal. They've invested well and have had a good return on everything that they've touched. They're billionaires now. Both of them." Grace asked if they were going to help her since she seemed to know so much about them. "No. They did want you to know that they have lots of money but that they're not going to come to your aid. I didn't ask them to, but they wanted to make sure that it was clear to you that they'd not even if they had twice as much money as they do now."

"I'll have to make sure that they understand that they'll help their mother or else. Where do they live? Also, I'll need a phone number for the two of them. Where are you going?" The stupid woman picked up her chair and left her there. She was tisking her as she walked down the hall. "Did you hear me? I want that information before you leave here. They're going to help me now or so help me they're going to regret being born to me."

"I do believe they already do regret that. You are a horrid excuse for a woman." She was still laughing when she went out the door. Grace sat there for several minutes before she realized a couple of things. She might well have bitten off more than she could chew right now. The second thing was she wasn't going to be going home anytime too soon.

"Christ, I hate people who are stupid." Smiling a little, she thought that most people were actually smart, but since they didn't do what she wanted, she called them stupid. Grace tried to think about what she was supposed to do now. Nothing came to mind, so she laid back on her cot.

They'll pay for this soon enough, she thought to herself. Especially her children. Not that she'd given them any reason to help her, she'd been treating them shitty since the day they'd been born. It had been fun for her. Who knew that they'd grow up to hate her?

"I guess I did." Laughing, she plotted her comeback in her mind. They'd not give her anything to write with, stating that it wasn't a hotel, nor could she have her own bathroom. Not that she really wanted it, but it was funny for her to demand things that were over the top.

~*~

Dexter wasn't sure that this was a good idea. He thought that the plan was perfect, but he didn't know enough about executing things like this to feel comfortable with what his part in this was going to be.

"You're going to be fine. Just follow me." He

asked her if she was sure that she needed him. He didn't want her to get hurt, but he wasn't sure what he was supposed to be doing, either. "Yes. I need you here. It's only a simple case of going in to see what has happened to the family that lived there. It's a man and a woman, and they've not checked in with their handler for several days." The couple had been moved with a new identity about six months ago. They'd been instrumental in bringing down a drug ring that had a great many people involved. "We only need to go in and see what's happened. That's it. Then we're out of there."

"All right. I can do that." He'd been practicing with his shifting to other things for the past several hours. He wished now that when they'd been ready to leave DC, they'd not answered their phone. She told him at the time that it wouldn't have mattered. They'd of come for them anyway. "I'm nervous about this."

"Yes, I can tell. If you were to fart right now, I'm betting that you'd have a stroke. Just trust that you can do this. It'll be easy." He asked her if she believed that. "I have to believe it for you, I think."

Once they were at the house, he did feel better. It wasn't as large as he thought it would be, but it was comfortable looking. Shifting to the mouse he'd need to be to get in, they were in the house in seconds when he could smell blood. However, it was old. Perhaps a week or so old. As he was about to follow Sunny to take a tour of the house, he saw a little boy.

He was perhaps ten or so years old. Shifter bear, too, but not full-blooded. As he watched the child making himself a sandwich, he turned to him suddenly. While neither of them moved, Dexter did shift to be his other self so that he could talk to the child.

"How did you get in here? I mean, how are you in here? You're here to get me too?" He said that he'd not been told there was a child in the house. "Yeah, that's my mom who made sure that no one knew that I was here. She hid me away all the time so that no one could use me against her. I think that didn't work out so well. She's dead. Has been for a while, but I've been afraid to leave here. These people came into the house when I was in bed, and I hid in my hidey hole to be safe."

"Where is your father?" He said that he wasn't his father but his uncle. That his mom and Don were sister and brother. "Do you know where your uncle is?"

"I hope he's all right, but I don't think he will be after what they did to my mom." Sunny joined them in the kitchen as her other self too. "You're pretty. My mom was too. She's in the bedroom down the hall. The men that came into the house, I could hear them, and they took my uncle away. Mom's dead. I don't go in there anymore."

"Good for you. Can you tell me your name?" Phil told Sunny that he was nine and that he was afraid that the men would come for him too. "We'll take care of you. Do you know who it was that came into the house to kill your mother?"

"My mom's dad. I never met him, but mom showed me pictures of him so that I'd know who he was when he came around. I don't call him grandfather. His name is Arnold Peterson. He was here when my mom was killed." Sunny went to the bedroom and returned a few minutes later. "What is going to happen to me now? I'm afraid that they'll come back here for me for some reason. They were all over the house when they — they killed my mom and then left with my uncle."

There was something there that bothered Dexter, and he wasn't sure yet what it was. The kid, he thought, was off about things, and it concerned him. But for now, he was following Sunny's lead in this.

"You're going to be safe. However, I don't want anyone to know that you're here. I'm going to —" There was a crash at the front of the house. Dexter pushed the child behind him as he let his bear take him. "Dexter, don't kill whoever it is. We need to get this resolved, and it won't help anyone to have the prick killed right now."

Making his way to the front of the house, he wasn't the least bit surprised to find several men in the room. They'd not noticed him as yet, which tickled him a little, so he watched them move around the room. They were obviously looking for something, so he sat down on his butt and kept an eye on them. While he didn't have any idea what they might be looking for, he wasn't sure at this point it was the boy. It was confirmed a few seconds later when the man who appeared to be in charge told them to find the money.

"I hid it in the closet down here when I'd come over. Now it's gone. It has to be here somewhere." They began tearing up the couch as well as knocking things off the wall. It was then that two of the thugs with Arnold noticed him. "What the fuck are you doing? I said to look—"

"There is a bear over there." They all stopped what they were doing and looked at him. Dexter couldn't help it. He waved at them, making sure that his claws were showing when he did it. When one of them waved back, Arnold hit the man upside the head with the gun that he had in his hand. "What the fuck was that for? He's bigger than we are. I'm not fucking with that."

While Arnold had been dealing with the man,

two of the men with him left the house. After telling Sunny what had happened through their connection, she told him that they were being picked up as soon as they got out to the street. Arnold hit the man again, knocking him onto the floor and out.

"Who the fuck are you? Better yet, shift." He could feel the compulsion, but it was so weak that he was easily able to ignore it. "Did you hear me, you fucking dick? I said to shift. Now."

Standing up, Dexter made his way to the older man. He didn't back off, which was stupid on his part but stared at him like he was still expecting Dexter to shift like he'd told him to. Getting right up into his face, Dexter roared, sending spit all over his face until he finally backed away.

"You're going to pay for that. Do you have any idea who I am? I'm the bruin leader for the whole entirety of the United States. I'm going to have you pulled before the board as soon as we're finished here." Sunny entered the room and told him that he was indeed finished here. "Who the fuck are you? I am not going to tolerate this kind of insubordination from underlings like you. You'll tell me your names, or so help me, I'm going to make you two suffer in ways that will haunt you every time you look in the mirror."

The room tightened then. It was as if all the air had been sucked out all at once, and the room paused. Then when his brother, Mark, appeared in the room, he felt the power of magic surround him as his breathing became easier. Whatever had happened, he had a feeling that Mark was just as surprised by it as he was.

The sandwich was halfway to his mouth when he looked at him. Mark, being Mark, smiled at him and waved. Dexter did the same, telling him what had happened since he'd arrived as well as the fact that the man in the room with them had proclaimed himself as Bruin King of all of the US.

"Well, that explains a great deal." He asked him what it explained. *"Why I was brought here. If someone does that and is joking, it's ignored. But when a person proclaimed himself as being king as well as threatening one of his family members, it was said that the magic that*

he had would take him to that person to...I guess you could call straighten them out. Were you hurt? Either of you?"

"He threatened us. Does that count?"

Sunny pushed Mark away when he hugged her. "Don't be all mushy right now. This man said that he was going to hurt me. While I could care less what happens to him, I need him to be around to stand trial for the murder of his son and daughter. Also, threatening his grandson."

"Grandson? Where is that little fucker? I want to see him. Right now. I have a good mind to kill that shit too." Sunny answered Arnold's question. "That is no reason for my daughter to keep him from me. She did that too. He's going to be just like me, and I love it. I will be able to raise him like I should have been able to do my son. Where is he? I'm getting sick and tired of having to repeat myself in getting you to do what I tell you."

"Perhaps because they know who the real king is." The man said it was him. Mark put out his hand only to have it slapped away by Arnold. The grin on Mark's face was very telling. "That isn't going to get you anyplace but in a grave. I'm not in the mood to fuck around with you today. I was in the middle of a nice lunch when you fucked up and had me summoned here. I am Mark James Cross. Bruin King of all the bears, shifter or born of all the country. You, Arnold Daniel Peterson, are hereby stripped of your magic. Stripped of your bear. All your magic will go to the rightful heir. You will stand trial as a human and suffer the consequences as they deem appropriate for your crimes against humanity."

Again, the room tightened, but the sound of Arnold screaming made it so much more tolerable to him. Dexter felt his bear stretch out under his skin. His claws, usually dormant unless he was in danger or, like earlier, having fun, pulled from his paw. Roaring again, this time with more effort than he'd ever had before, Arnold dropped to the floor with his belly showing to Mark.

"You can't do this to me." Mark, picking up his sandwich and taking a bite, said that obviously, he could as he'd done it. "You'll do as your told and give it all back to me. I'm a very powerful man, and

I— What the hell was that for?"

Sunny had kicked Arnold in the head. "You're an idiot. What do you think is going to happen now? You're just going to be given back what you didn't deserve and told, 'oh, go on with your life. Sorry about the mess up.' No, fucktard, that's not going to happen. I'm taking you to jail. After that's done with, you'll be taken care of by the bruin. Moron. Crusty Clumps like you give other clumps a bad name."

As he was being taken away, Phil joined them in the room. While the logistics of how Mark had gotten there were still unknown, he was going to take the boy back with him to his home to keep him safe. They'd try and find some family members that weren't going to jail to take him in.

"I'll look into what I can find. I'm not sure what, if anything, we can do, but we'll look into it for him." Mark hugged Dexter after he shifted and smiled at him before getting ready to leave with Phil. "Maybe he'll be a part of our family when we find him some lost aunt or something to take him in. He could be a mate to one of the others."

"You keep talking like that, and the others, as you called them, will hunt you down. Don't be making plans like that. They'll hurt you." Mark was still laughing when he left. Dexter looked at Sunny. "What now?"

"We find the money." They did too. It was in the closet right where the kid had told them he'd been hiding. Not only that, but they found guns, knives as well as a plethora of other weapons.

Chapter 5

There had been a cubby hole in the boy's bedroom that had the sacks of it stored away. There was no indication that the money had been used by the family. It was all bundled up in neat stacks. Even after counting it all, all the banned money was correct with the number that should have been in the stacks. Just over fifteen million dollars were found. In addition, they were able to find a book that belonged to Arnold, and the private diary of his daughter Jane had details about her father bringing cash over and hiding it in their front closet. Like she'd not notice it. She had called it blood money.

Arnold's diary was turned over to the FEDs.

However, Sunny didn't think that turning over the one that she'd found in Jane's bedroom would add anything to the trial, so she kept it for Phil. Jane talked about her love for her son and brother and knew, by what she said, that someday her father would come for the money she was taking from him and kill her for it when she wouldn't give it up. She had wanted it for her little family to run with after he was caught. However, it wasn't to be. There was more to the diary, but for now, she was only skimming it until she got someplace to read it in its entirety.

"I've located a grandmother to Phil. She wants nothing to do with him. Nor does any family members of Arnolds. They're blaming Jane and Don if there is a child, which they have indicated that it was a child of the unholy sex between Don and Jane. I didn't even argue with them but hung up. Now what?" Dexter told her that he had no idea. "Yeah, me either. He's doing well at your brother's home for now. But we have to do something for him."

In addition to the money that they'd found in the hiding place that Phil had been hiding in when people came over, they found a large stash of deeds to homes and land all over the world. Even about a dozen passports that had been updated as recently as two weeks before the death of Jane. They were the same pictures on all of them. However, the names were changed. However, it bothered him that there were only passports for Arnold and Phil. There were, sadly, none for Jane nor her brother to run with their father. Even though her diary had said, he had told them they'd be going with him.

"Who was it that they were hiding from? I mean, when people are put in a position to hide from someone, they usually don't have any contact with them. Was it their father?" Sunny told him that she was still waiting on a call from someone about that very thing. "Also, how the hell did they hide a nine-year-old from people coming around here all the time? There was a bedroom that he was staying in that was obviously a kid's room. Not to mention all the clothing that was spread all over the room. Someone should have noticed that, don't you think? Sounds off to me."

"Yeah, that's what I was thinking too. But no one is concerned other than they got a big shit fuck off the streets." He laughed at her name for Arnold. "I know. It did sound better when I was pissed off. There is something about the kid, too, that I'm being creeped the fuck out about. Like you said, how did anyone know that he wasn't in the house? How did he know that his grandfather had killed his mom? There are just too many things that—did you notice his face when I came into the kitchen with you? Like he was pissed off that I was there with you. Also, it wasn't until you left to go to the living room that I noticed that there was a big fucking knife there that was way out of whack for a peanut butter sandwich. I have to look into this. I did warn your brother to keep an eye on him that things weren't adding up."

Dexter's phone rang just as she was thinking she needed to get away from all this to think. "There is news about Phil. Do you want me to relay the message, or do you want Jamie to tell us both at the same time?" She said to put it on speaker. "All right, Jamie, we're both here."

"There is no record of Phil being born. Now I know that could be because of many things, but there is nothing that I can find. Nor did Jane, according to her autopsy report, have a child. Ever." Sunny looked at him, and he was suddenly afraid for his brother and Jamie. Dexter asked if they'd bring the boy here. "That's not necessary for the moment. Right now, I have several men on him. If you'd not mind doing this for me, Sunny can you come over and tag him or whatever it is that you do? I want to know where he is every second of every day."

"Of course. I can be there in a few minutes. Also, I don't know if you're aware of this or not, but I have Jane's diary. In it, she does mention Phil being her kid, but I've only glanced at it a little. I'll go over it better now that we have this information. What do you think is going on with him?" Jamie told them that she didn't have any idea, but she was a little leery of him the way he creeps around all the time. "That's it. I'm going to beat the shit out of the clump-it and see what I can find out."

"I'd rather you didn't. As much as I'd like to

know what is going on, I'm unable to breach his mind. Neither can Mark without hurting him, he told me. Whoever this kid is or whoever he is working for, they've given him something powerful so that no one knows what he's thinking about."

Jamie thought that it wasn't as easy as that. She knew a few people that she could have come and talk to him, and she was going to give them a call after going to tag the kid. They had been invited over for lunch with Mark and Jamie, and that was when she was going to make sure that he could be found at a moment's notice. There was something entirely off about this kid, and she wasn't going to let it go anytime soon. Whatever it was, she was going to figure it out and soon.

She was sitting in the office when Dexter joined her. After talking to a few of her friends, she was going to have one of them come and see what sort of magic the kid had. Dexter asked her if she was all right, and she told him that she wasn't sure. He agreed with her.

"I've spoken to Mark. He's not worried about

the kid, but he did suggest that while we're there for lunch, he commands the kid to tell him what the fuck is going on. I told him that I'd talk to you about it first. As we've been saying for the last several hours, there is something very odd about that boy." She told him who she'd spoken to. "A witch? I guess she'd have about as much luck as we have been having figuring this out. Do you think that he's been playing with black magic?"

"Conner does. He's been around for a very long time, and he said that he can spot dark magic as soon as he's close enough. Also, and this one sounds truer than anything we've come up with so far, he seems to think that the kid is in charge of all this going on and that he's been playing with adults to be able to get around. I don't know, but I'm about willing to believe anything at this point." Dexter told her that he was on board with that too. "There is something else that I've only just been made aware of. The only fingerprints on the knife that killed Jane are hers. I'm thinking that Phil had her kill herself by stabbing herself by using magic. I know that it sounds farfetched, but I'm not sure I want to discount it just yet."

"What about the money?" She told him that there were too many prints on them to make any kind of guess if it was only handled by Phil or Arnold. "Speaking of Arnold. He's talking with an attorney about what happened at the house. No one is going to believe him, of course, but he does say that he has information that could be used. I'm not sure what that would be at the moment, but we've been invited to go and listen in on the conversation that he has with his attorney. When I say invited, it was clear that they want us in the room as something other than what we are right now."

Lunch was a nice reason to go to the house. Phil looked like he was comfortable with what was going on around him. When she asked him how he was liking it here, he asked her if he could go back home.

"To what? There is nothing there for you. And even though you've been on your own for a few weeks, the FBI won't allow you to live in the house by yourself. Besides, it's being gone over with a fine tooth comb right now, and they're finding all kinds of things that are dangerous and illegal in the house." She saw it then. A flash of so much anger that she was taken aback with it. "Are you all right?" The smile was fake and didn't reach his eyes. Anger was still there, but it wasn't nearly as hot as it had been.

"Yes, I'm just fine. I'm going to go there and get some of my things." Even though it was a demand, she ignored it. Sunny told him that it was a crime scene and he wouldn't be able to take anything until they were done. "Well that's not fair. It's my stuff, all of it. Who do they think they're messing with?"

"I'm sorry. What?" Sunny knew the exact moment that he realized what he'd said. Telling her that he was really stressed out didn't cut it with her. "Just who are you that they shouldn't be messing with?"

"I'm just stressed out, that's all. I mean, I've lost my uncle and my mom all in—" She told him that Jane hadn't been his mother. Again the flash of anger. "She was too. It's on my birth certificate that she is. Why are you even looking into this stuff? I'm not going to tolerate you treating me this way. I know people that will make sure you keep your nose out of my business."

"Do you now? Well, I guess it sucks to be you because I know a great many more people than you do, you little shit. Who is it that you're paying off?" His nose started to bleed as he tried to fight her off. "I have friends here that are going to take you down, you mother fucker."

Her friend and witch, Amelia, appeared in the room and simply put her hand on Phil's shoulder. As the kid started screaming in pain, he began to morph into not just an adult but a man older than she knew Dexter's grandparents to be.

"What the fuck have you done to me?" She didn't bother answering him as his body was still catching up to his age. "You've ruined everything. Everything that I've worked my whole life for. Fuck you, bitch. I'll be back."

"No, you won't." As he disintegrated, his body turning to dust, no one at the table said a word. Amelia sat down in the chair next to where Phil had been and smiled at her. "He has been around a lot longer than I have. Also, he's been being looked for by the council of witches for some time. Killing him will make so many people happy from now on. I have information should you want it." They all said yes at the same time. But it was Sunny that asked the first question.

"He killed the people that he was living with, didn't he?" Amelia said that he'd killed Jane but not Don. "Is he still alive? I'd like to find him if that's possible."

"Sadly, he will not live much longer. I have sent some of the other witches that I know to get him and take him to the hospital. I'm afraid that he was tortured in a way that will not allow him to speak or to try and live a life that he would have without Phil in the picture."

"Did the others know? Jane and Don. Did they know that he was an elderly man that used black magic?" She said that they did in the end. "The supposed grandfather. What was his part in all of this?"

"A lacky. The boy/man had amassed a great deal of money by playing the role of either the boy or an elderly man. He'd been known to kill lesser witches for their magic, and that's a big no-no in our world. Also, due to the fact that he was semi-powerful, he was good at convincing people to do what he wanted of them. Like selling drugs and running prostitutes through houses. He also amassed a great deal of property over the years by acting like a poor little boy with no one to care for him so that he'd be taken in and then inherit all their worldly goods when they suddenly died."

"Christ." Dexter smiled when he realized something else. "If I know my lore about witchcraft, that magic will go to someone that killed him. Congratulations, Amelia. If anyone deserves it, that would be you."

"Nope, Dexter, it goes to the person or people, in this case, that helped in his demise. I was only there to take his magic. Getting him caught, that was all on you guys. You and Sunny will get not just his magic but after compensation to the ones that he injured —

if they come forward, it will all go to you. I'm glad for that as well."

The pain of something rolling over him took his breath away. Even as he fell backward in the chair, he could feel his animal tearing at him to get away from the pain. Just as he was letting the pain take him under, he heard his brother calling out for help as well. Dexter was glad. At least he'd not whined like a little baby.

~*~

Amelia gave the list of things that had been Phil's to the council. They weren't happy about the fact that it went to non-witches, but she didn't give a rat's ass. Phil, as they had wanted, was dead — which he was — and he wasn't going to be hurting anyone ever again.

"Once you found out where he was, why didn't you take care of him later when they weren't around." She told them that everything still would have gone to them as they were the ones that had found him. "You could have taken care that it didn't go to them somehow, couldn't you? I mean, that's a great deal of money, and we'll get no part of it as they're not witches."

"Is that what this is about? You couldn't pad your own money with his? Christ, no wonder it's getting more and more difficult to keep witches from turning to the dark side. At least they don't have to pay you guys when they make a little money on the side." Number two told her to be civil to them as they were her council. "Perhaps you are, but that doesn't mean that I have to agree with you. And as usual, I don't. The money has been given to them, and they're the rightful owners of it. It's done."

It wasn't, not really. The money was still in her possession, but the magic had been given to them. Unbeknownst to her, the entire family got the magic. There certainly was more than enough to go around. But she didn't tell them that nor the fact that she'd been given a boost too. If they had gotten their heads out of their asses and not thought about themselves for a change, they should have noticed it. As it was now, she thought that she could take them on and come out on top. Instead, she just let them talk among themselves about the injustice of the magic not coming to them. Then the five of them looked at her.

"We've made a decision." She was just pissed off enough to ask them what it was going to cost her. "Good that you're on board with us. We'll take half your monies—there is a great deal of it, we know and have your magic spread out between the six of us. That way, we are compensated for your mistake."

"What mistake would that be? The fact that you assigned me to make sure that Phil was no longer around, and I did that? Or the mistake I made in coming here to tell you the truth. Either way, you're not getting shit from me or my magic. Also, this might surprise you, too. I don't give a shit if you were compensated or not. Not that you deserve anything, but you're not going to get anything from me." All she did was lift her hand, and the five of them disappeared. "Christ, love a duck."

She'd been thinking that they needed to be out of a job when she'd done it but dropped to the floor when not only did they disappear from their thrones, but there wasn't anything left in the room at all. No filing cabinets, no monitors on the walls. The room seemed to be as swept clean as if a large wind had come in and taken it all away.

"Hello, Amelia." She didn't move from her position on the floor, not even to look up when she heard the woman speaking above her. "Oh, do get up from there and talk to me. It's been decades since I've had a conversation with you. Come now, get up."

"I didn't kill them, did I?" She still hadn't moved, but she heard the laughter and raised her head just enough to look at the woman standing before her. "Mom, you look amazing. What have you been doing with yourself?"

"Thinking. Get up, Amelia. You're going to make me get a crick in my neck like this, and I do need to speak to you." She stood up, and a table and two chairs appeared beside her. "We're having tea. Well I am. You're having some juice. In answer to your question, yes, they're all five dead. You killed them, so when you leave here, I'd expect to take yourself someplace where you can rest. Their magic, pitiful as it was, will come to you as well."

"I told you before, I'm fine with what I have now." They sat, and two under witches came to serve them. Not only were there several kinds of juice that she could choose from but there were fresh sandwiches and tea for her mother. "Why didn't you do something about the five of them before today? I told you that they were taking money that didn't belong to them. Why today?"

"You were here to make sure that I can't be blamed for their demise. You won't either. I think that everyone will be thrilled to know that they're dead. But with me being the grand witch, there would have had to be an investigation as well as an inquiry about shit. I'm not in the mood to go through all that. How have you been, darling?" She told her that she'd been great. "I'm so happy to hear that. I've been looking ahead — I know that you hate when I do that, but I've seen that you're to have a mate soon."

"You've said that to me before, mom. And my answer hasn't changed in all this time. I don't want a mate, and I have no need for one. I've seen how mates can destroy each other, and I'm not going to allow anyone to treat me less than I deserve to be treated. Like a person, not a dishrag." She told her that this man would never do that to her. "I'm sure you'd like to think that, but all men are dirt balls, and we both know it. Remember my father? He was jealous of everything you did. Even though he could have been better himself, he had too much fun making us feel bad for our ambition and worth."

"I will agree that he was a terrible role model for you, but not all men are like him." She said that most were. "Perhaps you would know that better than me as I rarely have contact with anyone but you. However, you've met his brothers. And their wives." She had to think about what she was saying and stood up. Twice.

"Mom, you don't mean that I'm going to be mated to one of the Cross Bears, do you?" Her mom smiled and nodded. "I don't think you understand how powerful they are in their own right. Not to mention the whole thing about me not wanting a mate."

"Sure you do. You just need to meet the right man. His name is Frazier. Such a good strong name. And he works with the elements of the earth. I'm not sure that he understands that he and the earth are a great deal alike, but you should see some of his work. Amelia, he's a brilliant man, and he loves the earth as much as you do." She didn't bother speaking to her mom about it. She knew her feelings about having a mate. "He and his family will need you in the future, child. He, along with one of his brothers, will be dreadfully murdered if you don't accept my word on this. As soon as you do, he'll have all the power he needs to survive what is coming his way."

"Just fix it so that he's all right without me being his mate. Mom, do you have any idea how much I've worked at being single." She nodded at her. "Then you understand why I won't do this. Just fix it up for them, and I'll go about my merry little way."

"I'm dying, Amelia. I want to die, but it's coming to me faster than I had thought when I made plans with the earth to bring the two of you together."

She asked her what she was talking about, fearful of what her mom might say to her. "I've been around longer than most of the earth, child, you know this. I am exhausted. My magic, while strong, is boring to me. Without a mate here, I have no one that I can depend on."

"You can depend on me. I come to you every time you call for me." She said that it wasn't the same. She had no one to share with. "Of course you do. You can share with me."

As soon as the words left her mouth, Amelia realized her mistake. Her mom took her hand into hers, and the magic poured over her. Even as she was overpowered with her mom's considerable magic, she could see the trouble that a man she thought was Frazier was going to be killed in. As soon as it occurred to her who he was, magic pulled him to safety along with his brother. Christ, she was going to have to sleep for years at the rate that the magic was coming to her.

Waking up, she was in her old bedroom in her mother's home. Sitting up, she sat there for several seconds until her head or the room, she wasn't sure which it was, stopped spinning. Finally thinking that she could move without falling over, she made her way into the hall to find her mom. Damn it, there was going to be hell to pay when she found her. Amelia found one of the under witches that worked for her mom.

"Where is she?" She bowed before her and told her that she'd been lain to rest. "No, I mean...what do you mean?"

"Your mother left you a message, my lady. Shall I bring it to you?" Amelia asked her to take her to her mother. "She is in the faerie garden not far from here. As per her magic, once she had transferred the magic to you, she was magically put into the garden where she could rest until eternity."

The garden was just where she'd been told it would be. There were fresh flowers, most of them bachelor buttons, her mom's favorite flower, around the small stone that marked her passing.

The stone was cold; however, she didn't take her hand away once she touched it. Asking her what she'd done to her, Amelia cried. Her heart was broken. Her mother was gone, and she'd been given the magic that had all been hers. Also, her title of grand witch.

Chapter 6

Frazier didn't speak to anyone as they made sure that Ewing was all right. He was still having trouble wrapping his mind about what he'd seen as well as felt when they'd been in the cave that— Frazier didn't let his mind go there for now. He was outside of the cave, and he was alive. As was his little brother.

"Other than a few scratches, you both seem to be all right." Nodding at Mark, afraid to open his mouth for fear of what would spew out, he didn't even look up when he said his name. "Something more than the cave falling in on the two of you happened, I'm assuming. Do you want to talk about it?"

A bubble of laughter spilled from his mouth, and he closed his lips tightly so as it would make him look insane. Mark didn't leave him but sat there on the ground with him. He did ask about the people that had been above them on the hillside.

"Both dead. Not because of the landslide they caused, but the TNT that they were using to make the mountain come down exploded before they were able to get away. They wanted to split the mountain in two to get to the treasures they were sure were in there." He then asked about the others in their party, the families that had been with him and Ewing. "All are fine. One has a broken arm. They said that you tossed the man out of the cave when he seemed to freeze up. Also, they have cuts and bruises that will fade. I doubt their memories of this will fade so—"

"There was a woman there. Not with us, but I saw her when I suddenly had this extra strength. Magic too. I could feel it even as I was feeling my last breath leave my body." He looked at Mark. "I should be dead. That big bolder hit me on the head, and I could feel my life slipping away then I saw her." Mark didn't say anything. Over the last several days, they'd all gotten some magic from the kid Phil. Playing around with it couldn't have prepared him for the surge that he'd gotten about an hour ago. "She's my mate. I don't know why I know that, but she's my other half. And she's a witch."

"Amelia? I don't know her last name, but she was just over to the house the other day." He said that was her. Frazier then told him what he knew about her. "Grand witch? I didn't know they were real. I mean, I would guess now that I have time to think about it that it makes sense. There would need to be someone in charge of their group."

"Coven. And her mother passed away, leaving all her magic to the two of us. Amelia is very old too. Several thousand years old. Much older than grannie and grandda are." Mark simply nodded. Is that all you have to say about that? I'm only here because her mother decided to give her daughter all she was, and it saved me and Ewing."

"Do you want me to be upset that you're still

here and not dead? Or that Ewing is all right? I'm sorry, but I can't do that. I'm thrilled to death about all of this. When will we all get to welcome her to the family?" Frazier simply looked over his brother's shoulder, and there she was. It was almost as if he could feel her coming near him. Mark turned to look as well and stood up when he did. "Hello again, Amelia. I'm so glad to welcome you to the family."

"My mother is dead. She died so that I could save my mate. I'm not very thrilled about shit right now." Mark laughed, and they both turned to look at him. "You think this is funny? That my mother is dead? I have news for you right now, buster. I'd gladly kill any one of you to bring her back."

"I'm so profoundly sorry for your loss, Amelia. But I will be forever thankful that you were able to save my brothers from certain death." He got down on his knees and put out his hands. "I pledge to you my undying gratitude. I am forever yours in anything that you wish from me. Except for harming my family."

"I don't want a mate. I don't...Christ, I told her

that I didn't want one so that I could go on with my life."

"You think that I'm going to make you do something that you don't wish? Or to ask you to do things that will make your life miserable? I'd never do that. You have it on the word of my grandparents' lives that I'd never do anything to harm you in any way." Amelia told him that she didn't believe him. "That's all right too. Painful, I won't lie to you, but I can understand you're not trusting me. We were thrust together by magic, strong magic too, if I don't miss my bet, and it'll take us both time to get used to it. But as far as you being able to go on with your life, Amelia, I have no intentions of taking that away from you. I might well enjoy hanging out with you, too, if you were to allow it."

She sat down on the ground and then stood up. A table and four chairs appeared beside them, and she told them to get up off the floor. In a matter of seconds, not only did another chair appear, but Jamie and Sunny joined them at the table.

They were in the middle of the woods with the

nicest table and chairs that he'd ever seen. With tea and if he didn't miss his bet, scones too. She told him that there was no reason for them to be uncivilized.

While she answered questions from the women, Mark took him to the medics that had been dropped in by helicopter. There was going to be a big fucking mess to clean up. The several hundred tons of rocks and other debris had traveled down the mountainside and didn't care what it took with it on the way down to the waterway below.

Frazier was sitting where he'd been told even after he was given a healthy check-up from the team. Amelia joined him when he was just thinking about how he was going to be taking the next couple of days off to rest up. He'd already been told that by Mark and the department head at the park that was what he was going to be doing.

"You're all right then?" He nodded at her, and she sat down on the stone that he'd been on. "I'm sorry for the way that I spoke to you. I'm not nearly as bitchy as I was. But with losing my mom today and knowing that you'd been in the cave when it went down, I didn't feel like I was supposed to be nice. Not that I am usually, but today had been a shitty day all around."

"I'm still reeling from the cave incident too. I can't call it a near-death thing as that's just too much for my mind to take in. however, I am sorry about your mother. I've never met her, but if she raised you, then she couldn't have been all that bad, right?" She laughed and said her mother had given up on her decades ago. "Yes, well, my grannie is still trying to get me to behave all the time."

"Mom passed her magic to me, well, the two of us. I'm not entirely sure what all that entails at the moment. Because, like you, it's been a lot to go over in the last twenty-four hours. However, you and your family are immortals. Your grandparents don't have to be. But they'll never be hurt or sick again. Even their bodies will be given a boost, and they won't hurt at all." He thanked her for that. "My skin feels like it's crawling over me I'm getting so much magic right now. How do you feel?"

"I've been trying my best not to think about it.

However, the strangest part is that I have knowledge about the magic I've been given and how to use it. Rules, too, on what I can't do with it. Is that something you gave me?" She thought it had been her mind as she didn't know some of the things that her mother had. "I guess I can see that. I have the next couple of days off to rest up. I'd like to use that time in getting to know you better. Nothing sexual or untoward but just getting general information on you."

"I'd like that. However, there is a huge list of things that I have to do with the witchcraft that my mother passed to me. Also, I killed the council just before I was to meet up with my mom. I need to figure out what I'm to do about that as well." He asked if he could help. "I'd like that. But we won't be around here while working. At least for now. Mom has…had several homes, and one of them, where she did most of her work, is where I need to be. I'd like it if you were to come along with me."

It was settled then. The two of them would work with the things that they'd inherited and get to know each other as well. Having a few days off didn't mean that he wouldn't rest. Getting the extra magic had zapped him badly. Not in pain, not really, but it working through his body was making him exhausted.

Telling his family where he was headed, he went with Amelia. They had the power to make themselves come and go as they pleased, but he was thrilled when she suggested that they take his truck. Like him, he thought that she was overwhelmed too.

~*~

Dexter had turned in his notice this morning. He was going to be on desk duty for the duration of the time he had left. Being both nervous and excited, he'd thought that his family would have been upset or, at the very least, try and talk him out of leaving such a wonderful job. They were so supportive of him that he began to think that perhaps he'd been whining too much, and they'd been sick of hearing about it.

"No, that's not it at all. But I've seen you in the building that you use to blow glass. You're an entirely different person when you're there. Relaxed too. I think that this is the best decision you've made in some time." Ewing smiled at him. "Also, I think you might well have cleared the path for the rest of us should we like to leave too. I don't, but I have a feeling that Mark isn't going to be around there for much longer. Especially if Jamie has a child."

"I have noticed that he's not as chipper when he goes to work lately. When he has his days off, he looks pissy when he returns. I love what I do for the park, I do, but I also know that—well, since that incident with Frazier that I want to spend time doing the things that are less dangerous. Less, I guess you could call it, making it so that I can get up every day without worrying if some kid is going to try and make a name for himself and blow me up. Or with what happened to Mark, not have to kill one of our kind because of entitled people."

Mark had been on a tour with a woman and her teenage kids. They didn't believe that bears or any animal out in the wild was anything but like they saw in movies. Putting out food for them to find, three bears attacked his group, and he'd had to put all three of them down. It had hurt him for days after that. The woman, she'd been charged with their deaths and had spent some time in jail over it.

After his brother left him to go on tour with a group of people, Dexter worked out his plans on what he was going to do to convert the barn he had been using into something that he could use year round. Usually, it was hotter than hell in there at any time, but it was getting the place heated up to use before he turned on his fires that would make him not want to go out and work. Also, he had some ideas buzzing in his head that he really wanted to make it work.

When his phone rang, he picked it up with the usual greeting that they all used and waited while someone on the other end talked to someone only they could see. As he sat there waiting, the woman in charge of the little shop that was also in the building where he was sat a bowl of fudge ice cream in front of him. He looked up at her, confused.

"A group of people came in and wanted some ice cream. When they figured out it wasn't free—I have no idea why they thought that it would be—

they handed it back to me to be thrown away. Then threw a hissy fit when I did indeed throw it out. That one I was still dipping when they huffed their way out. I heard that you were leaving." He told her his plans. "Good for you. I think that they built the mountain around your grandparents. They're such a lovely couple."

"Thank you. I think they're the greatest." Eating his ice cream, a perk he'd not counted on today, he fielded calls and made sure that any complaints or other things that came in were sent off to the right person. They usually had all kinds of complaints, so it was fun to send something off when it wasn't. Dexter looked up when Shelby, the woman who dished up ice cream, came into his office to tell him that the family was back. Putting his trash in the can next to his desk, he went out to see what all the shouting was about.

"Good. Someone in charge. That woman there, rather than just handing over the ice creams that were a mistake on her part, she tossed them out. Is this the kind of thing that I'm paying for as a person paying taxes?" Dexter told him it wasn't. "Good to know. I want her fired. That is a total waste of taxpayers like me, our money."

"Your taxes nor anyone else's pay for this park. It's funded by donations and other private funds." He said that wasn't right. He knew better. "So do I, sir. And since I live and work here, I think I might have a better handle on how this works than you. Rockefeller donated money — about five million to create the park. That's why it's free and open to the public. So that everyone can enjoy the park at their leisure. Now, Shelby here. She works for the park as a volunteer vendor. Her only job is to come in and sell some of the things the park has to offer. Like the other things in the park, it's bought for here, and we sell it at a profit so that the money can be used for things like ranger's salaries and other things that keep you safe while here."

"I think you have that wrong." One of the kids with the older man said that he was right and that he wanted his dad to let it go. "No. I'm making a point here, and I know that he's wrong. I won't have my taxes go to someone that thinks that they're smarter than I am about such matters. Now, I want her fired right now."

"No. I'm not going to do that. You have a good day." As Dexter was turning to go back to his office, the man grabbed him. Turning slowly so that the man did have time to remove his hand from his person. "Let me go, sir, before I have to do something that both of us regret. Shelby, call my brothers, please. Tell them what's going on here."

"You're going to do as I said and fire that woman over there. I don't care how you're treating me either." Stepping back when he was turned to the man, he reached for him again. Dexter, moving back out of the man's reach, bumped into a rack holding stuffed animals. Not that it mattered how far back he tried to maintain from the man, he would continue to advance, all the while shouting at him about firing Shelby. "Young man, you're going to be a heap of trouble if you don't do as I say. You mother fucker, fire that woman, and then we'll be getting all the ice cream we want. For free, you fucking prick."

The man's family went out of the store with the other patrons. Shelby knew her job, and when she was off the phone with someone, she hurriedly got the other customers out of the building. By the time the man reached for his gun this time, Dexter had no choice but to take him down.

Mark entered the room just as Ewing did. Guns drawn and pointing at the man that he had in a headlock. The first words out of his brother's mouth were to ask him if he had this. Then he asked if he was all right.

"I am. He got nasty with me when I wouldn't fire Shelby for having the nerve to charge him for ice cream." Dexter didn't take his eyes off the man that was continuing to scream at him but did ask one of them to come and take over. "I need to sit down. Right now."

He found himself in his office with his head between his legs. Never had a feeling of such rage and sickness washed over him like this did. When he lifted his head up, he thought it was Sunny pushed it back down. Dexter told her that she had beautiful toes.

"Don't be ridiculous right now. I'm upset with you — no, I'm pissed at you for getting hurt." He said he'd not been hurt. "Really? Then what do you call that large cut on your shoulder? My imagination? It's not. What the hell did he do to you?"

"I don't know. He did jerk me around twice, but I was so focused on keeping anyone else from being hurt that I didn't know that he'd hurt me. Is it bad, honey?" She said he'd heal. "You're such a compassionate person, Sunny. I feel so much better than I did before." She smacked him on the head. "You're very violent too."

"I was terrified when I came here to take you to lunch, and you were spread out on the floor with blood on you." Changing the subject because she did seem to be extra mean right now to him, he asked her about the family with the ice cream. "His wife said that he'd been acting out all day, but she said he'll do that sometimes when he's stressed. Like a toddler, she said. Then when the ice cream was tossed out, he lost it. I guess he drove them right back here to teach you a lesson. Apparently, this has happened to him before, getting out of hand like he did. The hospital where he was taken is checking him out thoroughly. His kids, of course, are mortified about what happened."

"I tried to reason with him, but that wasn't going to happen. I think that there was something wrong with him now that I have time to think about his behavior. Shelby said they were all fine and laughing until she told them what the price of the ice cream was going to be." Sunny let him sit up now, and he pulled her onto his lap. "I know I'm on duty, but this is calming my bear too. What do you we know about the family?"

"The kids were taken back to their hotel. Right now, no one is pressing charges against him in the event that he's off his noodle or something." He told her that wasn't nice. "I don't care. I'm stressed out myself. Anyway. The wife told the police while I was waiting on you to wake up that he used to be on antidepressants. She didn't have any idea how long it's been since he's taken them. I called bull shit on that, but before I was able to knock her around for the truth, one of the kids told their mom to come through with the truth. She wasn't helping their father."

"Good to know that someone is telling the truth. By the way, I'm going to have a crew out to the house tomorrow to work on the barn, my workplace." She nodded and stayed on his lap. "The house, I was told this morning in DC, is being updated too with security teams. And cameras are being put in. I didn't know you put my name on the deed."

"David said it would be a good idea that we're both on it. That way, we can either one of us make decisions on what is done to it." She got up and moved to the chair across from him, and he felt her sadness. "I hope you don't mind, but I spoke to your grandparents about being immortal. Neither one of them want to be hanging around forever. Even if grandkids start to come along. I guess they'd be their great-grandkids. Grandda said that even with the boost of being less sore all the time, he wants to die when his time comes. Grannie said the same thing. They're really in love, aren't they?"

"They are. I don't remember my parents all that much, but I know that they never acted like Grannie and Grandda do when they're together. I know that I shouldn't be upset with their decision, but I am sort of. More disappointed, I think. I'd love to see the two of them around any children you and I might have." Sunny said that she wanted children. "I do as well. As many as you'll have with me."

"We'll play that by ear." When Mark came into the room, he asked Sunny if he could have a minute with him. Not arguing with him like he thought that she would, he told her that he was joking and that she could stay.

"I'm stressed about this." Sunny told him that she understood that to spill what he had to say or not, she didn't want to have to hurt him. "I appreciate that as well. Mr. Traveler has passed away. He coded twice on the way to the hospital, and there was no saving him when he coded once he was there. His brain had been without oxygen for over thirty minutes when he was put on a ventilator as well as a heart pump. His oldest son, Paddy, is the one that pulled the plug not ten minutes ago. I guess his wife was his second wife and Paddy was his only child. The other two children were the second wife's kids."

"Christ, that's terrible. What was the cause of death? Have they figured that out yet?" It was Dexter that answered Sunny. "You know this how? I mean, how did you figure out he had a tumor on his brain that was killing him?"

"I told you that I knew that something was wrong. I remember now that I saw it on his brain. It had taken up most of the right side of his brain. He'd been warned about it. This trip out here was to be a lasting memory while he recovered at home. His doctor had told him that this was a bad idea. I didn't know it at the time, but now that I'm not in the middle of this, I saw what he was living with. Is this going to be normal, you think? Finding out shit after it's too late?"

"I don't know. I can't do that." Dexter nodded but didn't say anything. "Perhaps when you get used to what it is you're looking at or feeling, it'll be easier to figure out. However, it doesn't sound as if

Mr. Traveler was going to make it anyway if he was willing to disregard his doctor's advice. This trip was a bad move on his part."

It didn't make him feel any better that the man had disregarded his doctor's advice and had died. But he'd been as gentle as he could when the man had come after him. Also, he'd hurt him, too, and while it was starting to sting a bit, he was sure that the man hadn't realized what he'd done when he'd cut him.

When the end of his shift was finished, he decided to have dinner in town with his grandparents and Sunny. She was all for it and picked the elderly couple up and brought them into town with her. He knew that the two of them loved Chinese food, so that was where they were headed when grandda burst out laughing. Asking him what was so funny had him pulling off to the side of the road to listen to his story.

"Your mother hated Chinese food. I mean, there was nothing about it, not even plain white rice that she'd eat. However, your father loved it. To the point, I'm sure that he could have eaten it for every single meal. I have no idea what made me think of this, but one night your mother wasn't feeling well. Your dad, he went into town and brought home food for the three of us. They lived in the big house with us at the time. Anyway, your dad brings home a pizza, just cheese, for your mother, and she ate one slice of it. However, that didn't stop her from complaining about the smell of the food that the rest of us were eating. I think Mark was about five at the time. You couldn't have been much younger, maybe four or younger. But when your dad introduced you two to the food he was having, Mark picked up a bottle of sriracha sauce and poured it all over his egg roll. Like it was soggy, it was so covered in the stuff." Dexter waited for the punch line and was happy that whatever it was, Grandda was getting such a kick out of the memory. "Mark and you both loved it. It was hotter than hades, but you ate it. When your mother got up from the table to get a glass of water, we all thought she was done. So you, I love this. You poured more of the hot sauce onto a slice of the pizza. Your mother came into the room, picked up the piece that you'd just doctored and ate it. Holy crap, Dexter, I'm sure that everyone within a five-mile radius could hear her cursing. Your dad, he was laughing so hard that he fell right off his chair. I know that it's not nice to think that was funny, but I have to tell you, I have never been so entertained in all my life. And there you sat, upset that your momma had eaten your pizza."

They all laughed. Dexter still, to this day, loved hot food. And siracha sauce was still like ketchup to him and Mark. They'd even have contests on who could eat things the hottest. Sitting down in the restaurant also brought back memories of times when he was still in high school, and his grandparents came here to celebrate any kind of achievements that they had. While watching the two of them go over the menu, he couldn't help but notice how old they were looking. Even with the boost of good health, they looked tired.

"I love you both so much. I don't tell you that often enough, but I can't imagine anyone else raising us than you two." Grannie put her hand over his, and he kissed it. "I understand why you don't want to be around forever, but I know that every day that you're gone, my heart will break for not being able to see you every day."

"Oh, Dexter, you're the sweetest boy ever. We love you all to pieces, but we want to do this our way." He nodded, telling Grannie that he understood. "I'm so happy that you do. Both of you, you've brought such joy to our lives in the last few days that these will be memories that we'll take with us when we meet up with your parents again. I love you."

It was difficult to order after his heart was in his throat. Once they had placed their order, getting all kinds of appetizers for them to munch on, he settled into talking to them. If they were to go, he was going to get as many memories of them as he could. Taking out his cell phone, he took their picture. He was going to do more of that too. Get pictures of them for his own children to get to know them with.

Chapter 7

Sunny answered the call from David, but she wasn't happy about being awakened in the middle of the night. Going to the hallway, she told him that things had better be important.

"I've just had the most amazing sex that a woman can ask for, and you're fucking with my buzz. What the fuck do you want?" Silence at the other end made her regret being a bitch. "What's happened, David? Tell me."

He was sobbing so hard that she didn't understand what he was saying. Instead of asking him to start over, she reached out to his mind and searched for whatever had upset him. Once she found it, she sat down on the floor in the hallway and leaned her head back.

"I'm so very sorry, David. I can't imagine the pain that you're going through. Did your wife leave a note?" He was still crying about how she was gone when she looked again. There had been a note. "David, I'm going to come to you. Where are you?"

"At the house. The police are here, and they asked me if I could call someone. I don't know why you were the first person I thought of, but I would very much like it if you and Dexter were to come here." He cried again. "She's been dealing with breast cancer for a while now, and we all thought that it was in remission. But today, I guess she got a call from the doctor about her last exam. It had not only come back, but now it was in her bloodstream. Sunny, what am I going to do without her?"

"I'm on my way. With this magic that I've been given from—never mind. I'll be there as soon as I get Dexter up." As if she summoned him, he came out of the bedroom dressed. "We'll be there in a few minutes. Just wait for us, all right?"

"Yes. I'm not sure what I can do now. I just don't know what I can do now that she's not there." She wanted to tell him to buck up, but she didn't know the loss he was feeling. "Sunny, will you bring Dexter with you?"

"Yes. He's coming." Once they were both dressed, they simply popped into the kitchen of David's home. David was sitting at the kitchen table with something like the note in his hands. Dexter asked him if he was all right. When he stood up, clutching to Dexter like he was his lifeline, she went into the living room where the police, as well as the DC cops, were. It was a nightmare in there.

"Hello, Sunny." She shook hands with the man who seemed to be in charge. "David called us right away when he found her. I was about as shocked as I've ever been when he told me that Lily was gone. It took me several minutes of talking to him when I figured out that she'd cut her wrists in the tub and not just passed away from natural causes. Poor man. He's been crying off and on since we arrived."

"He told me when he called me that she

couldn't take it anymore with the drugs and pain."
He'd not told her that, but she saw it in his mind
when she read over what Lily had left in her note to
him. "My heart breaks for him right now."

"Dexter is with him now?" He said that he
wanted him there more than he did her, she thought.
"More than likely. I'm thinking that it's because
you're not one to be easy on a man. Dexter will hold
his hand until he doesn't need him to anymore. Then
he'll kick his ass." They both laughed. "If you could
tell Dexter to keep him in there for a bit longer, we'll
have her body brought out. It'll be easier on him."

She did that, telling him what they were going
to be doing. The officer asked her if she knew how
to get in touch with their children, if there were any.
Sunny told him they'd not had any children, but she
had to call Roger.

"You do that. I never thought of him needing
to know." Going into the dining room, she waited
for the president to pick up while she watched as
Lily was taken out of the house on a gurney. They'd
only put a sheet over her, for which Sunny was

glad for. The public didn't need to know what had happened. When Roger answered, she didn't bother apologizing about the lateness of the hour but told him everything that she knew right now.

"I'm on my way." She told him not to do that as the neighbors were out in force. "I need to be with him. David has been my friend for a very long time. Do you know if he needs anything? Something I can do for you until I can get to him?"

"He's going to need some time off. I'd say a month but perhaps longer. She was all he had, and I'm sure that he's going to be hurting with this for a good long time." He told her to consider it done for him. "Good. You might want to think about what you're going to say about this. She killed herself, and that's one of the platforms that you ran on, trying to reduce depression. I'm not saying that you should use this as a tool, but when asked, you might want to have something prepared. Like she was a great friend, and you can't imagine the pain she must have been suffering to go to such links. You can pretty it up for the press."

"I can do that. But you're right. I'm going to need to have something to say. That poor man. We'd argue a great deal, but we were the best of friends." She knew that as well. They were both a pain in the ass to her, but they were also the first to jump in when she needed them. They did the same for each other too. "I'm going to send a couple of my people over there to manage the neighbors. We don't need them saying things that they have no business saying. I just can't wrap my mind around what he must be feeling right now."

"He's devasted." Roger said that he'd be the same if it would happen to him. "All right. I don't know what you need to do on your end, but we'll be staying in town until he's in a place where he can be left alone."

After hanging up with Roger, she went to the kitchen. Dexter had made David a cup of tea and was talking to him about the trip they'd made a couple of days ago. Just nonsense talk but nothing too hard on the man. As David ate a couple of cookies, Dexter told her what the two of them had been speaking about.

"She had mentioned that she wanted to be cremated, and he isn't sure that is the way to go. I was just telling him that he'd know best about what she wanted or didn't want. I was just asking him if she gave a reason for that." David told him it was because she didn't think she had all that many people that cared. Sunny snorted.

"She was as beloved as you are, you dumbass." David smiled at her and thanked her for talking to him like she always did. "You do what you wish; however, I'd say that since she passed the way that she did, there is going to be a rumor mill running their mouths about what they think might have happened. You know that as well as I do."

"Yes, even if anyone had come here to see what had happened, they'd have their own version of what they saw. Doubtful, any of it was anything like it was." David stood up and dumped the tea into the sink. "I hate hot tea, young man, but I let you do it because you seemed to be needing something to do. I'm all right now. I am. I need to make arrangements for her funeral in the morning. I don't suppose I can count on you two to be with me?"

"Of course, you can. I've talked to Roger too. He's so sorry for your loss and will come to see you soon." David said that he'd like that too. "David, what is it you want to do now? I hope you're not thinking of doing something stupid. I'll kick your dead ass all over this place if I even have a hint about you wanting to join your wife."

"I had thought about it before calling the police. I did. However, I thought that if there was an afterlife, I'd not want Lily yelling at me for doing such a thing. She would have too." David looked at her. "You should have children now, honey. When things like this happen, having someone around that loves you unconditionally will make it seem all the better. I wish we'd had a dozen of them when we were younger."

Sunny looked at Dexter, and he smiled at her. Neither of them thought this was the time to tell him that they were all immortal right now. As they helped him pack up a few things, David not wanting to stay in the house tonight, they took him to their home there. As soon as he was in one of the many bedrooms, she called Roger again and let him know where he was. He said that he'd be there tomorrow for him.

The sun was coming up when they finally laid down. David was going to be here for the next couple of days, and they both thought it was a good idea that they stuck around here for him. When Roger showed up at eight, they were just making breakfast for themselves. David hung onto Roger much like he had Dexter. But Sunny knew that he was going to be just fine now.

After arrangements were made for Lily, David having decided, with the suggestion from Roger, that they'd have a service for her and then cremation. It was better than she could have hoped for. As she had said to him, people would talk, but there would be fewer rumors if they were actually able to see a body.

"There will be thousands of people coming, David. Might I suggest that you set up a place where, instead of flowers coming to you, that they can send money to a charity or something?" David thought that a wonderful idea. "Good. I don't want to tell you which ones to use, but I'd like to suggest two. The breast cancer society, as well as a hotline for suicide awareness. Neither of those charities has any kind of funding, and it might well help someone else when the need comes up for them."

"Yes, I love those ideas." Roger and David talked for about an hour. Then Roger needed to get back. "You'll come to the service, won't you, Roger? You and your missus. I know she never cared for Lily for some reason, but I'd like for you to be there."

"Nothing would keep me away." As soon as he left them, David went into the back yard. It was getting cooler now that August was about over, and he said he'd be all right alone. Dexter didn't want to leave him but seemed to be all right so long as he would stay where he could see him. He was like a big old mother hen with the older man.

"He said that he might have had a clue what she'd been planning if the tests came back the way that they had." Dexter watched David for a few minutes before he sat with her at the kitchen table. "David said that she'd been in a funk for a few days, telling him that she wasn't going to go through chemo again. I guess it really took a toll on her when she did it the first time."

"She was very sick. And they'd had plans to go on a cruise but had to cancel. I think that Lily never got over having to do that. But there wasn't any way that she was going to be able to do that and Chemo too." He asked her why they'd not had any children. "David was sterile from mumps as a child. And Lily had so many infections that it rendered her unable to hold a child for more than a few weeks after conception. They were giving and wonderful to the children around here, but they were also lonely, I think."

"That's a word that I've never used myself." The two of them laughed, and she felt better for it. "Speaking of children. You're coming up on being in heat. I'm not sure how I can tell that, but I can. Do you want to wait on children? I have no problem with that if you want to wait. But birth control or anything else will stop you from breeding if we make love anytime soon."

"I want you to tell me if you want to have children now." He said that as it wasn't his body, he couldn't tell her that— "do you fucking want to have a child with me or not? Don't make me have to pull your pretty dick off and beat the shit out of you with it. Tell me."

"I would love to see you large with our child." She smacked him. "What was that for? I answered you."

"No, you didn't. You said you wanted to see me fat with a baby but not a timeframe as to when you'd like for it to happen. So I'm going to ask you again, do you want to have a child with me at this time." He said that he did. "Now, was that so hard? No, it wasn't. I don't want to have to beat you to death each time I need an answer. As you have said to me a million times, it's my body. But the child will be yours too. If you have an opinion on having a baby now or later, then voice it. I swear to you, I can very easily tell you to fuck off."

"You don't have any trouble with that, that's for sure." He pulled her into his arms when it looked as if he was going to hit him again. Sneaky. "I would love to have a baby with you as soon as seven or eight months from now.

They talked about having children and what would need to be done at both houses to make them comfortable with a child or two around the houses. Just as he realized that she'd fallen asleep at some point while they were talking, David entered the room and sat across from him.

~*~

David wasn't sure how the young couple was going to take his decision. Actually, it was more like a request. He wanted to live out his days with them. He did love the two of them like they were his own children, and he and Lily had talked about how if they had had children, they wished them to be just like these two were.

"I won't cause you any trouble." Dexter said that he knew that. "I'm glad to hear that. In actuality, I'd like to live on your mountain forever. I know that it's a big leap from being a city boy all my life, but I need something, anything that keeps me from dwelling on what has happened of late. Not just with my Lily but everything. I want to get out of the city and go someplace where I can be effective."

"Are you talking about going to work for the Park Service or just working on the land? Either one of them will work for me. However, I'd have to talk to my family about it." He asked if he thought they'd object to that. "No. While they've never met you. If we say that you can be trusted with it, then they'll believe us."

"I need to hang out with others. You two allowing me to be here, it's made a difference for me. I know that Lily has only been gone for a few hours, but I think she's been gone from our life for some time. I know that I have as well. Just going through the routine of living. I want to do something more with my life." Dexter told him that he could understand that too. "Good. I wanted to talk to you about it as soon as I thought of it. You and Sunny speak about it and —"

"I was going to suggest the same thing. Neither of us has a father figure in our lives. Dexter does have his grandda, but our children won't have a grandda. You can come and be one for them. Perhaps you can change a few shitty diapers." Sunny sat up and looked over at David as she continued. "You don't have to return here when we do. But I think the entire family will be happy to have you in their lives. I know that I will."

Dexter told him that he'd talk to his family and get back with him. David went to the room that he'd been given and laid down on the bed. The room, not at all like his own home, was friendly. Like someone had taken the time to make it homey. His rooms, the entire house, had been decorated with the idea that politicians would be staying in the rooms. David knew that there were no pictures of things that he liked anywhere in the place too. He decided to talk to his wife.

"I'm going to move in with Sunny and her mate. I think that with you gone now, I'm going to need some support." He rolled to his back and looked up at the pretty paper that was there to enjoy. "Sunny will kick my ass for even thinking this, but in those few minutes that I was with you when I found you, all I could think about was taking the knife and ending my life too. Now I'm going to be a grandpa to their children."

David cried a little, telling his wife that he wished that she'd spoken to him before doing this. He even told her that he understood her reasons, but it still hurt him to his heart that she'd left him behind.

"Once the funeral is over, love, I'm going to go to the mountain with them. And once I get your cremains back, I'll take a part of you on all my adventures." He didn't know if that was tacky or not, but he and his Lily could tell each other anything and everything. "If I had to do it over again, I would have done just what we did. Being with you, it was the best years of my life. But I'm not just yet ready for my life to end. Not yet. I'm going to live, and I'm going to do things that we always talked about doing. I might even talk someone there into taking me fishing."

He spoke to his wife for most of the afternoon

into the evening. Getting up, stretching his body out, he knew that he was going to have to get into better shape than he was now. David found that he was really looking forward to it too.

After finding the kitchen occupied with the cook and butler, he told them what he wanted to eat. He was given a good deal more than he thought he could eat but was happy when the two of them talked about the house when Sunny's grandparents lived here. He was laughing at her antics when the couple joined him in the kitchen.

"The funeral home called here. I figured you were taking a nap. But I told him what you had decided and he thought that a wonderful idea to have a service for those she had contact with. Also, he said this would give him time to find a bigger venue for the service." He asked Sunny if she thought that many people would come by. His wife had been out of his world for some time. "That's it exactly. They'll want to be there for you. Anyway, Roger called too. He said that if you wanted to have the service on the White House grounds or even in one of the bigger buildings, to let him know. He's thinking that it will be a huge affair too. With his permission, I gave his number to the funeral director so that they could work it out."

"Thank you for that. I'll have to go by the house and get her something to wear. She'd murder me in my sleep if I were to just toss anything on her." David cried a little, thinking about what he'd said. "She might well have put something out for me to take to them. I didn't think to look around."

"There is a blue dress hanging in her closet that has all the things that she wanted to be cremated in. That will work for her, don't you think?" David agreed with Sunny. "All right. I'll pop in there to get it soon and take it to the funeral director. There are still police at the home, just making sure that things are safe until you get back."

"I'm not going to go back there. Not even to pack up, if you don't mind." She told him that she was there for him whatever he wanted to do. "I want you to do everything that needs to be done if you don't mind. I'm feeling pretty good right now, knowing why she did this, so I don't want to go back there and have second thoughts about what I've been thinking about. Lily would be upset with me, I think, if I were to do that."

"You mean that she'd kick your ass?" he laughed and nodded. "I believe that you're right on that. Yes, if you and Dexter would do that for me, I'd be beholden to you. I've only just now decided to sell the house too. Do you want it?"

"No, this one is large enough, I think." He laughed with Dexter. "I have a couple of friends that I can talk to about putting your house on the market, but we'll wait awhile. You might change your mind about it, and that would be all right too. But we don't want to give to the rumor mill any more juice than they're going to make up on their own."

He decided that they'd wait a couple of months or more to deal with the house. However, he was going to have someone go in and clean it from top to bottom so that it would be ready. Not this week, but soon. David knew that he was making sound decisions, but he also didn't want to rush into things that he could and should wait on.

"There are some insurance policies that I need to take care of too. I only just remembered. I have no idea how to go about taking care that Lily's wishes are met." Dexter told him again that they had plenty of time. "Yes, I suppose you're right. Things just pop into my head, and I feel better when I can voice the things that I'm thinking about. You two are good for me."

That night when he went to bed, he was thinking about how many things that he had to do before the funeral. Nothing major, not really but things that he knew he'd have to take care of.

When he got into his bed, he noticed that there was a picture of his wife on the bedside table. He'd have to thank Sunny for getting it for him. Picking it up, he told Lily what he'd been doing today.

"I don't want to not talk to you nightly, honey, but I don't think I'll be able to move on with my life if I do this daily. I know that you'd kick my bottom. I think of you with every decision that I make." He wondered if he was moving too quickly to get on with his life. "Do you think so? I'm not pushing you aside, but I need something in the future to look forward to. I never realized until today that we were stodgy. Not my word, love but Sunny's. She asked me if we had a pattern that we followed once I was home for the night, and I realized she was right. We did the same thing nightly. I loved working out crossword puzzles with you. Then watching the nightly news, but when I sat down to do it tonight, it wasn't the same. It hurt me. I'm going to work around that for a bit before I become a zombie, as Sunny called me."

He thought of all the times Sunny had come to their home for dinner and how she'd had him and Lily laughing so hard by the time she left. He needed more of that, he thought. Laughter in his life.

"I'm thinking that you have been preparing me for this for some time, haven't you? Since you were in remission that last time. Shaking me up with different things and telling me that I'd better not be hanging around your grave expecting you to come up and talk to me about your day." She had, several times over the last few months, told him not to dwell on things that he could no longer control. "Roger has given me a year off with pay for my grieving. I'm going to take it, and when I'm ready, I'm going to quit the job. A younger person should have been doing it."

Rolling to his side, he let the tears fall as he thought of his life without his wife. He'd not be lonely, he realized, nor would he be unhappy. But he would miss her. Telling her good night, he let himself fall into a peaceful slumber and saw his wife there.

"Am I dead too?" she shook her head at him and pointed to something in the yard where they were. "Honey, are you upset with me?"

"Never. And while she won't tell you, I spoke to Sunny two weeks ago when I thought that I'd have the tests back and they'd be nothing either of us wanted to hear. But come look, Davey. Look what you'll be able to see when the time is right."

The two little babies were bundled up tightly in a blanket of sorts. Reaching down, the one that took his finger was suddenly older and sitting on his lap. Looking at himself with the child, the other one came to sit on his other side. He pulled a book out of the air and started to read it to them. As he closed the book, he saw that the children were bigger even now. High school to perhaps college age.

"You'll love them like they're ours, Davey. And you'll tell them all about their mother and father too. Even me." He said that he'd like that, even as the children were handing him children of their own. "Davey, please tell me that you'll take the gift that they offer you and be around forever with them. Those little ones will love you so powerfully that you won't ever feel pain again."

"I can do that." As he settled back in his dreams, he smiled in his sleep. "I will love doing that for us both."

Before You Go...

HELP AN AUTHOR

write a review

THANK YOU!

Share your voice and help guide other readers to these wonderful books. Even if it's only a line or two, your reviews help readers discover the author's books so they can continue creating stories that you'll love. Log in to your favorite retailer and leave a review. Thank you.

Kathi Barton, a winner of the Pinnacle Book Achievement Award and a best-selling author on Amazon and All Romance books, lives in Nashport, Ohio, with her husband, Paul. When not creating new worlds and romance, Kathi and her husband enjoy camping and going to auctions. She can also be seen at county fairs with her husband, who is an artist and potter.

Her muse, a cross between Jimmy Stewart and Hugh Jackman, brings her stories to life for her readers in a way that has them coming back time and again for more. Her favorite genre is paranormal romance, with a great deal of spice. You can visit Kathi online and drop her an email if you'd like. She loves hearing from her fans. aaronskiss@gmail.com.

Follow Kathi on her blog: http://kathisbartonauthor.blogspot.com/

www.ingramcontent.com/pod-product-compliance
Lightning Source LLC
Chambersburg PA
CBHW020620180626
46810CB00007B/2865